THE 12TH DATE

by Mia Reign Miller

Table of Contents

Chapter One
NEVER Land

I stood in the doorway, keys in one hand, a half-zipped overnight bag in the other. Peter was on the couch, in the same green pajamas he'd worn all day, headset on, eyes glued to the TV. The Lost Boys were yelling something through the speakers, but I couldn't make out anything over the laughter and digital gunfire. I'd been standing there for a few minutes, second-guessing my decision, hoping he'd notice. Hoping he'd stop me. But he didn't look up.

"Peter," I finally called out.

He didn't even flinch.

"Peter."

This time, my voice cut through the room. He glanced up, annoyed, then pulled down one side of his headset.

"Babe, we're in the middle of a raid. Can this wait, like... fifteen?"

Of course it could. Everything could always wait. Our relationship, my dreams, our future—always fifteen more minutes.

"I'm leaving," I said.

"Okay. Can you bring back snacks?"

I swallowed hard. "No, Peter. I mean, I'm leaving."

That made him pause. His eyes flicked to the overnight bag slung over my shoulder, finally registering it. He looked up then—eyes wide.

"What? Why? We're good."

"We haven't been good in years."

He dropped the controller. "Come on. We can spend time together. I just need to get to the next level of this game, then I'm all yours, I promise."

I shook my head. "That's what you said at breakfast. And lunch. It's five p.m., Peter. You're busy building forts while I'm trying to build a future with you. You're focused on game levels. I'm focused on *our* next level. That's the difference."

"I can change."

He stood now—suddenly close, suddenly serious.

He knew how to turn it on, a knack for putting on a show when it mattered most. The soft voice, the wide eyes, that earnest expression that could probably charm just about anyone into believing him.

And God, he was beautiful. Tall with broad shoulders, that perfectly messy, tousled dark hair, and lips that still knew exactly how to smile in a way that disarmed me.

A grown man, yes, and dreamy as hell on the outside. But on the inside, he was stunted. Not in a hidden, wounded kind of way.

No—he wore his immaturity like a badge of honor, like growing up was the one rule he'd sworn to break. And yet, right now, he looked at me like he was really ready to change.

But I wasn't falling for it. Not this time.

He tried again. "If this is about the ring, I've been saving. I've been looking. Just... not yet, okay?"

Not yet. The national anthem of our relationship.

He reached for my hand, and for a moment, I let him. Because this was the part of me that still wanted to believe him, that still thought he might surprise me.

"Don't go," he said. "I'll change. I'll be better. Just give me time."

Time? I'd given him over fifteen years. We were high school sweethearts, for heaven's sake. I'd spent all these years waiting for him to grow into someone he kept promising he'd be.

He dragged a hand down his face, like this was all just so hard for him.

"I'll figure it out," he said—really going for the award this time. Best Performance by a Bullshitter in a Leading Role.

But no. He wouldn't figure it out. Not really. And I'd already shrunk myself down too many times to fit inside this version of love.

I pulled my hand away. "You'll be fine," I said. "You've got your boys."

And I left.

Because he was never going to grow up.

Never going to propose.

Never going to choose me over the next shiny thing, the next hangout with the boys, or the next one-thousandth new friend.

I was done with never. I was done with him.

My name is Jane Norwell. And I was so done with Neverland.

Chapter Two
Just Plain Jane

The cold Snow Bridge air hit my face the second I stepped out onto the stoop, that crisp, just-before-Christmas kind of air. The sky was already dark, but the city sparkled under strings of fairy lights and radiant storefronts. Snowflakes drifted down through it all like confetti, blanketing the streets in a soft white layer.

I used to dream about living in Manhattan, with its bright lights and Broadway at the heart of it all. But I never left Snow Bridge. It was home. Only a few miles away from Manhattan, and truthfully it was the perfect compromise. A beautiful city with its own rhythm and charm. Parking, though, was definitely not part of the charm. But that's just life in most of New York.

My car was parked a few blocks away. I'd moved it earlier for street sweeping, and of course, the only spot I could find was practically in another zip code.

I raised my arm for a cab, but just as I stepped toward the curb, Rapunzel rushed past me and hopped in. Her braid got caught in the door as she slammed it shut, her long golden hair cascading down like a waterfall.

The cab pulled away. Gotta love New York. I didn't even have the energy to be mad. Honestly, watching that braid drag through the slushy streets of Snow Bridge felt like karma doing its thing.

Screw it. I could walk a few blocks. I wrapped my coat tighter around me and trudged into the winter wonderland. My breath puffed out in little clouds as I passed rows of brownstones adorned with festive wreaths.

The crunch of snow under my boots was lost in the buzz of the neighborhood—honking cars, distant chatter, and the low thunder of the L train rumbling somewhere overhead. A bell jingled as the door to the cocoa shop swung open in front of me. Little Red stepped out, balancing a steaming cup in each hand. She gave me a quick nod, like we'd passed each other before. Maybe we had. Inside the shop, Hansel and Gretel taped a sign to the inside of the window that read, "Gingerbread Houses and Candy Cane Sale," one of the best little holiday deals in town.

I turned the corner and nearly tripped over three blind mice who spilled out of the toy shop, scattering gift cards as they barreled straight into a lamppost. One of them squeaked something about "holiday crowds" as if that explained everything. I guess they weren't wrong, the city was always busy this time of year. Snow Bridge went all out for Christmas, and people came from everywhere just to catch a glimpse of the magic.

But once you looked past the holiday sparkle and Christmas carols, the city still had its everyday grind. People had jobs to get to and errands to run, and not everyone had a magic carpet to get around town. Nearby, a wolf in a peacoat stood at the bus stop, grumbling under his breath about the bus running late. Up ahead, traffic slowed as a goose waddled into the crosswalk and, midstride, laid a glittering egg. A gnome in a reflective vest scooped it up and carried it to safety.

"All clear!" he called, waving us through like it was just another day on the job.

I continued down the block, squeezing through a line of shoppers held up by two dwarves arguing over mitten prices at a sidewalk stall. Above them, a tiny fairy with iridescent wings fluttered, handing out tiny snowflake-shaped coupons.

As I moved past the line, I spotted a coachman waving traffic around a pumpkin carriage that had stalled in the middle of the street. I used to dream about owning one of those. Now I was just glad I never followed through. Those things were always breaking down. Not that I could really afford one anyway. I shook my head and kept moving. That's when I caught a whiff of something sour as a grumpy troll stomped past, slapping a parking ticket onto a double-parked pickup truck.

Up ahead, a man with donkey ears and a tail was unloading boxes from a candy-striped van, muttering something about back orders. Judging by the way he was parked, he'd be next if he didn't hurry.

A blur of motion pulled my eyes skyward, where a witch zipped past on a broom, bundled in a parka and carrying a Trader Joe's bag slung over one shoulder. My feet were already starting to ache. Must be nice to fly.

She sailed right over the deli, where a full-blown snowman contest had popped up, transforming the plaza into a glittering winter showcase. Just another extravagant display in a city that never did subtle.

The Queen of Hearts, in full royal red attire, was directing a group of cheerful card soldiers as they sculpted a series of heart-shaped snowmen. Nearby, a group of tourists clustered together, gasping and snapping photos, as the Snow Queen, draped in a glistening cloak, flicked her wrist to conjure intricate snowflakes that spiraled through the air in whimsical shapes.

Snow Bridge buzzed around me. Christmas lights glowed in the bodegas. The city didn't slow down for heartbreak. It didn't pause just because I'd finally walked away from the only relationship I'd ever known. And somehow, that felt like a gift.

The city kept moving. And so would I.

Even on the coldest winter days, the spirit of joy and hope could still warm the heart. I took a deep breath, and that same just-before-Christmas air filled my lungs, crisp and cool and laced with possibility. I kept walking, and just as I was starting to settle into the rhythm of it, I passed the *Mad Hatter Hat and Tea Shop* and knew I was close to my car.

Fifteen minutes later, I was still in Snow Bridge, but just far enough to feel like another world. I finally pulled up to my sister's place. A whole house. An actual house, with a front walk, a porch swing, and its own driveway. So different from the cramped blocks I was used to. At least I didn't have to circle for parking anymore.

I could already smell the cinnamon before I reached the front door. I barely had time to lift my hand to knock before the door swung open on its own—classic, and there she was, my sister Celeste, looking red-carpet ready, draped in a silky, champagne-colored wrap dress that shimmered in the light. Her hair fell in soft, flawless waves around her shoulders, perfectly in place, and she wore the quiet confidence of someone who made perfection look accidental.

A tray of fresh cinnamon buns floated beside her, accompanied by a bottle of wine uncorking itself in midair.

"Here. Comfort food," she said, offering me one of the buns, still warm and glistening with frosting. "You did it, didn't you? You finally left him."

I nodded, collapsing onto the couch. "Thanks, but I'll take the wine."

I'd held it together all the way here, through the snow and the bustle of the holiday crowds. But as soon as I walked through Celeste's door, it all started to slip.

Celeste handed me a glass of wine and sat beside me. "Are you okay?"

"Mostly. But I mean… I wasted all my good years on him. What am I supposed to do now?"

"Hey, stop that," Celeste said. "You're amazing, and you still have so much to offer."

Of course she'd say that. Celeste had the kind of relentless optimism that made everything seem possible. But that was because she could do everything.

She had magic, sure, but even without it, she was the kind of person who just functioned. The kind who glided through life with a luminous presence and effortless charm. A flick of her wrist, and the kitchen was spotless. Sweaters folded themselves in midair. Dinner prepped itself. Emails answered. Calendars updated.

Me? I couldn't even get through a load of laundry without losing a sock. And I've never been the kind of person who lights up a room. I didn't shine like that. I was background, a wallflower. No magic. No glow. Just plain old Jane. Sometimes I couldn't believe we were related. But we were, and although Celeste didn't truly realize how different things were for ordinary me—I loved her, and I wouldn't trade her for anyone.

Before I could dive deeper into my thoughts, her husband, Henry, wandered in, wearing a crisp button-down shirt and blazer, holding a coffee mug that read, "Knight in Shining Suit." He kissed Celeste's cheek and gave me a gentle smile. Trailing behind him was Princess Butterscotch, their gold-and-white collie, a name that could only have come from their five-year-old daughter. Princess Butterscotch padded over to Henry's side with loving loyalty, then flopped by his feet like she owned the place.

Then came the thud. A clatter followed, and from the hallway, a frustrated little voice called out, "It was supposed to be a prince!"

In marched the five-year-old in question, my niece Penny, a pint-sized whirlwind with a determined look in her eye. One hand clutched a wand, the other held a spell book tucked under her arm, and a small frog clung to her ankle.

Celeste held out her hand. "Your spell book. No unsupervised magic, remember?"

"But I was only trying to help!" Penny protested, kneeling to scoop up the frog, her eyes wide with earnestness.

She held it out to me, the little creature blinking up at me, innocent and hopeful.

"Kiss it," she instructed, her voice full of conviction. "He'll turn into a prince, and you can marry him."

My heart melted at her sincerity. Five years old, so full of hope and belief.

"Oh, sweetheart, I love that. But even if you *could* turn him into a prince, that wouldn't mean he'd want to marry me. Magic can't make someone fall in love." I leaned in and kissed Penny's cheek.

Henry gave me a parting nod as he tapped Penny on the shoulder. "Let's give your mom and Aunt Jane some privacy," he said, guiding her down the hall, the frog still cupped carefully in her hands.

Princess Butterscotch trotted after them, her fluffy tail swaying like she had important business to attend to. As they disappeared down the hall, Celeste sighed.

"Sorry. Kids hear everything."

I shrugged. "It's fine. Her heart's in the right place."

My phone chimed. I glanced at the screen, "Speed Dating. 8 PM Tonight. Your reservation is confirmed."

I stared at it. "Did you—?"

Celeste gave me an innocent shrug, but there was a mischievous twinkle in her eye as she refilled my wine. "What? Would you rather kiss the frog?"

I narrowed my eyes. "You're sneaky."

"I'm efficient," she said. "Come on, it's twelve days until Christmas. You don't want to spend it alone, do you?"

"I won't be alone. I have you guys."

"Of course you have us," she said. "You always have us. But it wouldn't hurt for you to have a *him*, too. Just go on the dates. One of them might be fun. One of them might be awful. But at least you'll have tried."

I stared at the screen. It's not that I hadn't dated in the past fifteen years. Of course, there were a few rebound dates here and there when me and Peter would break up from time to time. But it had been a while, and I'd be lying if I said I wasn't nervous about putting myself back out there.

But how did I expect to start a future with somebody if I wouldn't even give myself a chance to meet anyone?

Celeste was right, it couldn't hurt to at least try. And I had to admit speed dating made sense. A chance to meet people, get a feel for who they are right away without dragging things out with the wrong ones. I'd already done enough of that with Peter. The more I thought about it, the more the dread gave way to curiosity. Maybe it wasn't such a bad idea after all.

I took a sip of wine and sighed. "Fine."

Celeste raised her glass. "Now that's the spirit… but we definitely need to do something about that outfit."

I looked down at my sweatshirt. I'd packed an overnight bag, but unless the dress code was "hoodie and emotional baggage," I was completely unprepared.

"I packed sweats and break-up leggings," I muttered.

"Don't worry," Celeste said. "We'll glam you up."

Celeste led me into her bedroom, which looked like a lifestyle spread, part glam dressing room, part sanctuary. With the snap of her fingers, the closet doors opened and a dozen hangers glided into the air, forming a floating carousel of fabric and sparkle.

A deep green dress floated forward, glittering faintly in the light. She gave it a once-over, then raised an eyebrow.

"Too Emerald City!" She flicked her wrist and the dress returned to the closet.

One by one, dresses floated in front of me—black velvet, midnight satin, gold chiffon. I shook my head at each one. They were all completely out of my comfort zone. A slinky red number hovered into view. It was long and silky, with delicate spaghetti straps and a neckline that flirted with scandal but stayed just on the right side of classy. It was beautiful, show-stopping in a way I rarely let myself be. Celeste didn't even wait for my opinion.

"Perfect," she marveled.

"It's... bold," I said.

"It's gorgeous," she countered. "And it's been dying for a night out."

"I don't wear red."

"You do tonight."

I shook my head again, but Celeste was already floating the dress toward the antique privacy screen in the corner.

"Behind there," she said. "No arguments."

I hesitated. "I really don't think—"

"Just try it on."

With a dramatic, exaggerated sigh, I finally slipped behind the screen to try it on. When I stepped back out, she gasped. The dress fit just right, like it had been perfectly tailored for me. The color was bold and unapologetic, giving my skin a radiant glow and making me feel braver than I actually was.

"Wow," I breathed.

"Told you," Celeste said, already summoning accessories.

A jewelry box flew open, and out floated a pair of gold drop earrings that shimmered with every movement. Her makeup drawer slid open, and a powder brush swirled across my cheekbones with the precision of a top-tier glam squad, while Celeste fluffed her fingers through my hair, transforming my sad strands into voluminous waves. A tube of lipstick uncapped itself and hovered, waiting patiently for application.

Perfume sparkled through the air, misting as I turned in a final spin. I stepped into the heels waiting for me, and in an instant, the look was complete.

"Ta-da," Celeste said with a bow. "Behold, ten-minute transformation."

I smiled, staring at my reflection—red dress, red lips, hair in place, and heels for a change.

"I look like someone who has plans."

Celeste raised her glass. "You do."

Chapter Three
Once Upon a Table

The valet opened my door and I stepped out carefully, definitely not used to walking in heels. At least valet had saved me the walk, and I had arrived with five minutes to spare. Not like I could miss the big sign, "Once Upon a Table." I smirked at the name, as if sitting down here could somehow guarantee a fairytale ending. But secretly, I was kind of hoping it might live up to it. I took a deep breath and headed toward the door.

Inside, it looked like someone had taken an old jazz lounge, sprinkled it with fairy dust, and added mood lighting. Velvet booths. Low candlelight. A harpist and pianist played quietly from somewhere near the back, their melodies drifting through the room, soft and alluring.

A man in a sharply tailored coat and a deerstalker cap stood by the host podium, a magnifying glass held to one eye as he studied a leather-bound reservation book. His nametag read "Holmes." He looked up as I approached, one brow raised.

"Hm. Red dress. Somewhat nervous energy. Lipstick recently applied. You've either just robbed a cosmetics counter or... you're here for speed dating."

I nodded. "Guilty—of the speed dating part."

He smiled and snapped the book shut. "Elementary, my dear, not Watson. Welcome to *Once Upon a Table*. Right this way, Jane."

He led me past a row of white-linen tables, the space trimmed in garlands and gold ribbon that framed doorways and wrapped around banisters. A small ensemble played near the back, lovely harp and piano notes mingling in the air, underscoring the clink of glasses and quiet conversation. We reached a secluded section reserved for speed dating, with small, intimate tables tucked into cozy alcoves, each already occupied by women. Name cards marked each spot, Aurora, Cinderella, and others I didn't dare look at for too long. I didn't need help doubting myself.

It appeared I was the last to arrive.

"The game is afoot," Holmes said, gesturing to Table Four, where my name shone brightly in elegant cursive.

Across the room, the men clustered by the bar, each wearing a nametag pinned to his chest. Some stood tall, while others were already sweating through their collars.

Holmes gestured to my seat like it was a throne.

I sat. Breathed. Reminded myself I wasn't trying to meet The One. I was just trying to start over. One awkward, overly-cologned conversation at a time. I'd given pep talks to classrooms full of kids without breaking a sweat, but that was different. They were kids. This was a one-on-one conversation with a stranger, and somehow that felt harder. But it shouldn't be *that* hard... right?

The little bell chimed, and I sat up straighter, adjusting the front of my dress. First date in a while. No pressure.

And then he walked in:

Date #1: Prince Charming

He arrived as if the room had been waiting for him. His coat caught the light just so, his cufflinks sparkled like tiny crowns, and every step exuded calibrated charm. Heads turned. Conversations paused. Even the harpist missed a note.

He crossed the room like he owned it, then bowed and took my hand delicately in his own.

"Charmed," he said, kissing my hand. "Prince, though most just call me Charming."

"I'm Jane," I managed.

"Enchanting," he said, sliding into the seat across from me with a practiced flourish.

We chatted—or tried to. Every time I began to answer one of his questions, he cut me off with a story of his own. The gala he hosted last weekend. His apartment renovation. His mirror placement, and how he'd had to replace all the lighting in his penthouse to get the right golden glow at dusk. "You'd be surprised how unforgiving LED lighting can be on bone structure," he said, pulling out a compact mirror for the second time.

I took a bite of the food that had arrived—Prince Charming might be striking out, but the chef was a hit.

"I can tell you're intimidated," he said smoothly, setting the mirror down.

"Not at all," I said. "Just full."

"Of admiration?"

"Of risotto."

He smiled like I was the adorable one. "You're fun. Most women just cry when they meet me." He adjusted his cufflinks, admiring their gleam. "Too much majesty all at once. You're holding up well."

I took a sip of water. He was beautiful, no doubt. Charming in all the ways that didn't quite require substance.

When the bell chimed, he stood, kissed my hand, and gave a slight bow. "You've been an absolute delight," he said. "A perfectly lovely mirror to reflect me in."

And before I knew it, he was gone, already charming the next poor soul. My first date back, and I'd spent most of it watching someone fall in love—with himself.

The chair across from me barely had time to cool before the next one arrived. He glided in, black-on-black suit, slicked-back hair, and skin so pale it gleamed like porcelain beneath the candlelight:

Date #2: Dracula

His eyes were dark and beautifully haunting, like velvet shadows.

"Jane," he murmured. "It's an honor."

I blinked. "Hi."

Smooth, Jane. Real smooth.

His voice was low and luxurious, the kind of voice that didn't just charm, it glamoured.

He didn't talk much at first. He just listened closely, tilting his head like every word out of my mouth was something rare. He never broke eye contact, and I couldn't decide if that was deeply respectful or slightly hypnotic. Maybe both.

I asked where he was from.

His lips curved into a slow grin. "Old places. The kind that forget you before you forget them."

I laughed, even though I didn't fully get it.

His lips curved deeper, as though savoring the sound. "I like your laugh. It's warm. Familiar. Like something I once dreamed."

Okay. That one hit a little.

He leaned in. "Do you believe in fate?"

"I'm not sure about fate. But I've felt things… things I can't explain. Little nudges. Like something's pulling me somewhere."

"Maybe I've been following the same pull."

His voice wrapped around me, cool, precise, and a little dangerous in its cadence. And he looked at me as if I were the answer to something ancient he'd been searching for. My mind raced with a million thoughts, each one more thrilling than the last. This is crazy, I told myself. He's just a guy. But he didn't feel like just a guy. He felt like an obsession waiting to happen.

He asked for my number when the bell rang. I hesitated, only for a second. Then I gave it to him because… yeah, he was exactly my type. The kind of fantasy I used to create when Peter made me feel invisible. The kind of guy you probably shouldn't give your number to. But sometimes, curiosity is louder than caution.

Date #3: Frankenstein

He was kind, polite, and surprisingly gentle for a guy who looked like he could tear a phonebook in half. He handed me flowers that looked freshly picked—possibly from a cemetery. A little droopy, a little thorny, but still sweet. I wasn't sure if he'd given flowers to the others, but either way, I thanked him, feeling myself brighten at the gesture.

And then it happened—the dreaded ex talk. Only three minutes into an eight-minute date, and he was already calling his ex a witch. At first, I thought he meant figuratively. But no—he meant literally. Green skin. Broomstick. West Coast coven. Said she was intense, volatile, emotionally unpredictable. Claimed she once turned his therapist into a toad mid-session just for validating his feelings.

"She couldn't help it," he added sadly. "She was born that way. Fire, spells, emotional unavailability…"

He went on. And on. And on.

It was clear he wasn't over her. Every compliment came with a qualifier.

"You're way more grounded than she was."

"She never listened the way you do."

"I can already tell you're safer."

I sipped my drink and nodded at the right moments, but deep down, I knew the truth.

He didn't want a date.

He wanted a therapist with cleavage.

Date #4: The Scarecrow

He was sweet. Thoughtful. A little clumsy, but in a way that felt more endearing than awkward.

He said he enjoyed birdwatching, stargazing, and long walks. He talked about his love of autumn, hayrides, pumpkin patches, and his longing for a partner to share those experiences with, and hopefully build a life together.

We discovered a shared love of dancing, though he admitted he wasn't exactly great on his feet. But hey, it's the enthusiasm that counts.

He wasn't smooth, and he was a little scatterbrained, but he was kind and attentive. He wasn't trying to be charming; he just was.

I liked him. And when the bell chimed, I almost wanted to ask for five more minutes. We swapped info. I didn't know if anything would come of it. But for the first time tonight, I kind of hoped it would.

Date #5: Pinocchio

He was stiff in the beginning, his posture so straight and still that I could've mistaken him for a mannequin. His shoulders were tight, and his hands were folded neatly on the table like he was about to give a PowerPoint presentation. Not nervous, exactly. Just… overly polished. Like someone trying really hard to be what he thought a real man should be.

But the more enchanted martinis he drank, the looser he got. Unfortunately, so did the truth. He slouched in the chair like a marionette whose strings had been cut. His stories unraveled fast. He said he was 38. Two minutes later, he said 40. I tried not to judge—I mean, who hasn't lied about their age?

But the stories kept shifting. First, he said he lived alone, then mentioned roommates. He claimed he was an architect, then later said he worked in construction.

It wasn't just the lies. It was the ease of them. The way he said one thing, then the opposite a minute later, and just kept a straight face, like it was the most natural thing in the world.

This man lied like he breathed.

By the end of the date, I wasn't sure if anything he'd said had been real.

Date #6: Robin Hood

He walked in wearing all green. I hated that my mind went straight to Peter, but the resemblance was hard to ignore. That lopsided grin, that air of playful defiance, that glint in his eye, like life was just one big game.

To his credit, he asked questions and listened. We talked. But the more we talked, the more I realized, we were on completely different wavelengths.

He lived for the rush, archery, axe throwing, jousting. Game nights with the boys. Pool. Darts. More darts. I'm all for fun, but there has to be something more—a goal, a direction, growth.

I asked if he had any long-term goals—he laughed.

"Long-term? I'm more of a live-in-the-moment kind of guy."

Of course you are. No plans, no structure, just vibes. Peter 2.0. Same charm. Same energy. Slightly better boots.

He never once mentioned anything romantic, or even remotely relationship-oriented.

It wasn't that he was a bad guy. He was actually nice. Energetic. Charismatic, in that just-one-more-round-with-the-boys kind of way. But I'd been down that road before. I didn't want to spend another relationship competing with poker night, or coming in third behind darts and adrenaline.

A year ago, I might've convinced myself that being chosen second or even third still meant being chosen.

But I've grown. You shouldn't have to compete. Either it fits, or it doesn't.

And this? Didn't.

I didn't need someone with a life plan carved in stone. But I needed more than another night of "just the guys." I wanted someone who was open to building something real with someone, even if it wasn't all figured out yet.

Date #7: Dr. Jekyll

He introduced himself as Henry. He was clean-cut and dressed like someone who had a closet full of pressed shirts and an actual relationship with starch. A grown-up. That was the vibe.

"I'm a surgeon," he said when I asked. "Neurosurgery."

"Wow. That must be intense."

"It can be. But it's worth it." He shrugged. "Saved a life today, actually."

There was a sincerity in his voice that caught me off guard. I melted a little, not just because of what he did, but because of the way he spoke about it. There was no ego, no bragging, just facts.

He didn't ask invasive questions, and he didn't stare like he was trying to figure me out.

He was thoughtful and a good listener. I found myself telling him about my students and how we were rehearsing for something special this Christmas. I even mentioned Penny's latest "magic mishap." He laughed—not to be polite, but like he genuinely enjoyed hearing it. He made me feel like it was okay to be myself. And just as my guard finally slipped, the bell chimed.

Before I could even process it, his pager buzzed. He glanced at it, then apologized. "Sorry. Emergency surgery. I've got to run."

"No, it's fine," I said. "Really."

As he stood, he paused. "This has been really nice," he said. "Would you want to meet again?"

That caught me off guard in the best way. I nodded, smiling. "I'd like that."

He smiled back. "Same time tomorrow?"

My heart did a small, hopeful somersault. "Sounds perfect."

Then he was gone. But I couldn't stop smiling. It was a perfect ending to a strange, unexpected night.

Seven men. Seven stories. Some amusing, some surprising, a few that checked the right boxes, and a few that just… weren't for me. But this? This one felt different. It felt like a new beginning, the start of something special.

I didn't know what tomorrow would bring, but for the first time in a long time, I was hopeful.

Hopeful for tomorrow.

Hopeful for the future.

Hopeful for love.

Chapter Four
Clair de Lune

I was just here last night. Same restaurant, same gleaming sign above the door, "Once Upon a Table." I had smirked at the name last time. But tonight, heading into my second date with Dr. Jekyll, my face lit up at the sign, almost believing that love wasn't so impossible after all.

I entered the restaurant, and it was just as I remembered it—same candlelit tables and twinkling garland curled around the banister. The same ensemble serenading softly in the background. The restaurant hadn't changed, but something in me had. I wasn't nervous the way I had been yesterday. This was different. There was no name card waiting for me this time. No bell, no time limits. Just me, him, and possibility.

Jekyll was already there, seated at a quiet two-top near the back, tucked beneath the gentle shimmer of the overhead light. He looked polished, poised, and just as attractive as I remembered. He stood the moment he saw me.

"Jane, it's really good to see you," he said with open delight, stepping around the table to pull out my chair.

I sat down, murmuring a soft thank you. And as I settled in, the room around me faded. No distractions. Just a man, a woman, and what I hoped was the start of something real.

The conversation flowed easily. He remembered that I was a performing arts teacher and even asked how my family was doing. He was thoughtful and engaged without anything feeling forced. I didn't feel like I had to prove myself or play it cool. I just felt... seen.

He stood to head to the restroom, and I asked what he would like to drink, just in case the waiter came while he was gone.

He smiled. "Just water, please. I don't drink."

I nodded, and he walked away. Sure enough, as soon as he disappeared, the waiter showed up.

"One enchanted cabernet for me. One ice water for him," I said, almost giddy.

The waiter left, and I sat there, basking in the simple pleasure of a date going well. The lighting was warm, the conversation flowed easily, and the ensemble began to play *Clair de Lune*—one of my favorites. I leaned back in my seat, letting the music wash over me like a dream I didn't want to wake from.

The drinks arrived, but still no Jekyll.

A few minutes passed. Then another song. Then another. The familiar melody of "Pachelbel's Canon" rose up, pulling me into the moment and distracting me from how long he'd been gone. For a while, it felt like the kind of romance I'd always imagined— delicate music, candlelight, and a sense of possibility in the air.

The waiter returned, this time to take our dinner order.

"He just stepped away for a minute," I said, glancing toward the hallway.

I placed my order. Jekyll still hadn't returned.

By the time the next song started, the thrill had begun to wear off. I was just about ready to send out a search party when he finally came back. Only... something was different.

His smile was still there, but it didn't reach his eyes. His movements were sharper now, more rigid than before. He sat down abruptly, not looking at me right away. His eyes scanned the room like he was somewhere else entirely.

"I was almost starting to think you weren't coming back," I said, half-joking.

"Why wouldn't I?" he replied. "You're hot."

I blinked, taken aback. That wasn't how he'd talked last night. Last night, he'd been reserved and respectful.

But maybe it was just a compliment? I hid behind a sip of my cabernet.

He glanced at the table, frowning at his glass of water.

"Water?" he asked, lifting the glass like it offended him.

"That's what you asked for," I said carefully.

His brow furrowed. "Sure. Of course." He scoffed as if I'd said something ridiculous.

He flagged down the waiter like he was calling a dog. He ordered a "real drink," gave the waiter a smirk, and murmured something about how if you want something done right, you have to do it yourself. He narrowed his eyes at the water, like it proved something about me. Or about him.

"No offense," he said, letting out a sharp breath through his nose. "But that's why I always handle my own stuff. I can't afford mistakes. I save lives. What I do matters."

He launched into a monologue about all his achievements and skills and asked if I "even know how to do CPR?"

Before I could respond, he was already snapping at the waiter who had returned with his drink. "I said Merlot, not move slow, G!" he barked, loud enough to turn a few heads.

The waiter muttered an apology and backed away, but Jekyll didn't even look at him. He just stared at me. He asked about past relationships, career plans, my views on politics. All valid questions,

I guess. But it wasn't what he said—it was how he said it. His tone sharpened, and his questions shifted from curious to pointed. His views and goals changed at the drop of a dime. Last night he said he wanted to slow down, meet someone real. He'd talked about kids and settling down someday. He said he'd just gotten out of something serious and was trying to be intentional. Tonight?

"I don't really do long-term," he said casually. "It's just a made-up rule people cling to because they're afraid of being alone."

I paused. "Is everything okay?"

He stared at me, unblinking. "I liked you better when you didn't talk so much," he said, then reached for his drink.

My stomach twisted. I should've left. I knew that. But part of me was still clinging to the man who pulled out my chair and made me feel seen. That version of him couldn't have just vanished... right?

I tried to salvage the mood, to steer the conversation back to neutral ground. But the energy had shifted, and there was no getting it back. Somewhere, somehow, the guy who made me feel special was gone. And someone else—someone colder, more guarded—had taken his place.

When the check came, I offered to split it, maybe out of habit or reflex, who knows. He slid the check across the table, his card already tucked in the sleeve. The name on it was Jekyll.

But the name he signed?

Mr. Hyde.

He walked me to the lobby, gave a stiff nod, and pushed through the doors, disappearing into the Snow Bridge night. There was no warmth between us. He didn't ask to see me again, and I didn't ask either. I stayed inside a moment, coat folded over my arm, replaying the last hour in my head. *What the hell just happened?*

Back in Celeste's guest room, I slipped out of my dress and into sweats. My makeup was off, my hair tied up, and every ounce of optimism I'd carried into the evening had gone the way of my mascara—smudged, streaked, and quietly wiped away. I didn't even realize how much I'd let myself hope until it was gone.

Celeste knocked once and let herself in, already in pajamas, holding two mugs of tea.

"I heard you come in. You're back early," Celeste said, handing me one of the mugs.

I took it without meeting her eyes. "Yeah."

She studied my face. "That bad?"

I gave a small nod, still not looking at her.

She sank down beside me on the bed. "You want to talk?"

I stared at the tea, the steam curling up into the silence. "He was perfect. Until he wasn't. It was like he flipped—like I was talking to a completely different person."

"Some people can only keep up the act for so long. It's a good thing he showed you who he really was sooner rather than later."

"I know. I just wish I hadn't gotten my hopes up."

"You're allowed to hope," she said. "That's not weakness. That's bravery."

I gave a faint laugh. "Tell that to the part of me that feels like an idiot. I wish you could just… wave a wand and help me find someone."

Celeste tilted her head.

"I know that's not how magic works," I said quietly.

"I wish it was," Celeste said.

We sat in silence for a minute, both of us sipping and not needing to fill the quiet. That's the thing about sisters. Sometimes they know what to say. Sometimes they know not to say anything at all.

We said goodnight, and eventually I climbed into bed and turned off the lamp. I tried to sleep, *tried* being the key word. I lay in bed, staring at the ceiling, going over every moment of the date, still trying to figure out where it all went wrong.

Then my phone lit up on the nightstand, softly glowing in the dark. A new text waited for me.

Dracula: "Are you awake?"

I stared at the screen, but I couldn't bring myself to answer. Not because I wasn't interested. Not because I'd given up on finding someone before Christmas. But because I was tired, mentally and emotionally.

Tomorrow was Monday. Back to work. Back to reality. I'd let myself get wrapped up in a fantasy these past few days. But tonight, I didn't have it in me to keep hoping. I just needed quiet.

Chapter Five
A Place Like No Other

Monday morning came faster than expected. Back to reality. Only today wasn't a typical day. Just a week ago, I'd been working through choreography notes and rehearsal schedules in my cramped little classroom, with its linoleum floors and buzzing fluorescent lights. Now I was driving toward the gates of the Northpole Palace, a place so enchanting and otherworldly, it looked like it had been lifted from the pages of a storybook and brought to life.

I'd lived in Snow Bridge my whole life and still never made it past the gates. Just outside the borough, tucked between Snow Bridge and Manhattan, the Northpole Palace—home of Nikolas the Great, was as famous as it was exclusive, like the White House or Buckingham Palace. Technically open to the public, but only if you had the time, the ticket, or the connection. I had none of the above. Until now.

Nikolas—yes, that Nikolas. Santa, Saint Nick, the man in red himself. The one behind the sleigh bells and midnight chimney landings.

He inherited the Palace from his father, Nikolas. And his father before him—also Nikolas. The name isn't just tradition: it's legacy, a line of men, each chosen not just by blood but by something deeper, something magical.

It isn't automatic. When the time comes, the next in line must sign the Charter of Inheritance. With a single signature, everything shifts. The Palace accepts them, the reindeer answer, the sleigh flies for them and no one else. The magic of the season transfers in full, recognizing the new keeper as though it has always known them.

To the outside world, he's beloved. Part celebrity, part royalty. But here, he's something far greater—the heartbeat of this place. A legend who carries centuries of magic and meaning. The embodiment of the stories we grew up on. A legacy wrapped in velvet and wonder.

Every year, the Palace hosts the Northpole Holiday Benefit Production—a multi-act performance event dedicated not just to raising money for charities, but to fueling the spirit of giving. The performances fill hearts, lift spirits, and spread joy across the world. It's the most-watched broadcast of the year, powering everything on Christmas Eve, from the sleighs to the reindeer to the deliveries, and most importantly, the belief that kindness can still make miracles.

Each year, a different district is selected for the opening act, and one school within it gets the honor to perform. This year, it was mine. My sixth-grade musical theater class would be opening the show.

Today was orientation for performers, crew members, and instructors, everyone helping set the stage for the holiday benefit. Tomorrow, the kids would arrive, wide-eyed and sugared-up, ready to rehearse on-site for the first time.

It was every child's wish to visit the Palace and every performer's hope to perform here. It was truly the stuff of dreams. And if I was being honest, I was starting to feel the enchantment too. After the disaster of a weekend I'd just had, it felt good to return my focus to my students, helping them shine. And now, to do it here, in the most magical place in the city, felt like an even greater gift. A chance to remind them their voices mattered and that even the smallest stars deserved their moment to light up the stage.

A crowd of onlookers had already formed outside the gates, phones raised, excitement written across their faces as they waited for a glimpse of something or someone wondrous. The closer I drew, the more excited I felt too. Something in me lifted. Something I thought I'd lost was flickering back to life—hope.

I arrived early and followed the emailed instructions to the outer gate. The Palace wasn't just big, it was sprawling like a royal campus, as if Versailles met Disneyland at Christmas. The gates loomed ahead, massive ironwork framed in curling black and gold filigree, dusted with last night's snow. Arches curved over the entrance, where a security elf with a clipboard checked my ID, handed me my badge, and pointed me toward staff parking.

I parked and joined a line of arrivals, all of us brimming with energy and nerves. Some looked like seasoned pros, maybe returning performers, costumers, or tech crew. Others, like me, were stepping through the gates for the first time. A handful of us had been brought on to support the Palace's seasonal programs and, more urgently, the upcoming benefit. I might've been the only teacher in the bunch, but I wasn't alone. Everyone here had a part to play in pulling off the biggest holiday event of the year.

A candy-striped shuttle pulled up to the curb. I slid into a window seat near the front, securing my badge to my shirt.

"Welcome to the Northpole Palace," the driver said cheerfully. "It's cold outside, please keep the windows up and your arms inside the ride at all times."

The shuttle pulled forward, and it felt surreal just to be on the Palace grounds. I couldn't believe I was really here, and I couldn't wait for my students to see it too, so they could take it all in for themselves. We began winding through the estate.

"Now, we won't see everything from the outside," the driver added, "but I'll point out a few highlights before your official indoor tour."

We passed an enormous toy workshop, its outer walls lined with tall, frost-trimmed windows that gave a perfect view inside.

Beyond the glass, the scene was mesmerizing. Conveyor belts whirred, tools sparkled, and elves in green jumpsuits zipped between workstations like clockwork.

"To your left," he announced, "is our Toy Division. Fully functional, highly enchanted, and never—not even once—behind schedule. Our elves are trained in every toy category. And yes, they do unionize."

Laughter rippled through the shuttle.

"To your right, you'll see the ReinDash Logistics Hub, where packages fly faster than you can say 'two-day shipping.' It's one of our busiest wings, especially in December, but we're open year-round. Deliveries go out around the clock and not just toys, but care packages, surprise gifts, wish-fulfillment parcels, groceries, and last-minute necessities. If it lifts spirits, we deliver it."

We passed a stretch of snowy runway lined with rolling slopes. He gestured toward the window. "That's the reindeer flight deck, where they stretch their legs and take to the skies. Yes, they fly. And yes, they're adorable," he added with a wink in his voice. "Most of the herd's resting now. They're nocturnal by nature, most active at night to stay in sync with their Christmas Eve flight. So if you're only working days here, I'm sorry to say you might not catch a glimpse." He paused, then added with a grin, "Unless there's sugar involved, then they'll show up in seconds."

By the time we reached the main Palace steps, I was somewhere between overwhelmed and enchanted. The shuttle let us out in front of tall golden doors. They creaked open slowly, towering and heavy like the gates of a long-lost castle. I stepped through and stopped in my tracks. It was too much to take in—the size, the radiance, the exquisite beauty. I felt small and lucky and strangely at home, all at once. The grand foyer opened before me, its sheer expanse stealing my breath the moment I stepped inside. High ceilings soared overhead, and gleaming floors reflected the light from lavish chandeliers, their crystals scattering little fireflies of color across the room.

Guests from my shuttle began to peel away—one greeted by a uniformed staff member, another swept off by a friend's excited wave. Their voices echoed faintly, blending with the velvety notes of a brass quintet playing a slow, jazzy rendition of "Deck the Halls."

And deck the halls they did. Garlands of lush greenery, dusted with frost and woven with glimmering ornaments, lined the hallways. Wreaths graced the doors, their bows and sprigs of holly festively bright. In the center of the foyer rose a towering Christmas tree, its branches adorned with crystal baubles and jeweled trinkets that glittered like starlight. Pine and peppermint hung in the air, mingling with the scent of freshly baked pies, carrying a fragrance that seemed to hold Christmas itself—richer and more vivid than anywhere else.

Soon, more staffers appeared, clipboards in hand as they called names and guided guests into small groups. One by one, they were whisked down different corridors, their footsteps fading into the distance. Others waited in the cushioned lounges, each nook flanked by a roaring fireplace whose flames danced merrily, casting candlelight that beckoned you to sink in and stay. I hovered instead, too restless to sit, my nerves humming even in the Palace's inviting warmth.

As I gazed around in awe, my eyes were drawn to stunning ice sculptures that sparkled in the ambient light. Their intricate designs seemed frozen in time, untouched by the Palace's warmth, as though enchanted by some mystical spell. I lingered on the frozen beauty, entranced, until I realized how quiet the room had become—the guests had all been guided away.

I stood near the sidelines, unsure where I belonged. I was part of the school district showcase—the "special guest" performance, but no one had called my name yet.

That's when she appeared. Gliding into view like a vision, she didn't carry a clipboard like the others. She carried a wand.

She wore a breathtaking gown of shimmering lavender, the fabric flowing around her like a soft cloud. The gown's voluminous layers swept down to the floor, each fold glistening with sequins that caught the light, casting iridescent hues.

Her hair cascaded in lavender curls down her back, nearly blending with her dress, while a crown of silver crystal flowers rested atop her head.

She held a silver wand, a perfect extension of herself, its tip set with a glowing gem, radiant and beautifully luminous.

Her voice sparkled, just like everything else about her. "Jane Norwell?" she asked softly.

I froze for a second, unsure whether to shake her hand or wave—or bow, maybe?

"Yes, that's me." My voice caught a little, coming out thinner than I'd hoped.

She smiled, bright and reassuring.

"Sorry," I added quickly. "First day jitters."

"No need to apologize," she said. "I know I look a little…
much. Comes with the job. But don't let the glitter fool you—I'm
really not all that fancy."

She leaned in slightly, lowering her voice like we were sharing
a secret. "A little sparkle helps when you work in a place like this.
But I'm your ally—your Fairy Guide Mother. Just a fancy name
for orientation guide. You can call me Guidemother, or Gwenna
if you prefer."

My lips tugged into a smile. "Gwenna is perfect."

"Wonderful. We'll start with a tour so you don't get lost, or
worse, wander into the sleigh launch zone by accident. Come along!"

She led me past a set of glass doors, sunlight spilling through
as we stepped into a central atrium.

"This," she said proudly, gesturing with her wand toward the
open expanse, "is the Event Courtyard. Enchanted all year round.
Open to the summer breeze, open to the winter flurries—where
the snow stays frosty, yet your toes stay toasty."

Gwenna's eyes brightened as we walked on. "Further down is
where we house our magnificent companions."

We rounded the corner of the courtyard, and the reindeer
stables came into view, with polished wood and the sweet aroma
of fresh hay filling the air.

"Our reindeer have the option of indoor-outdoor living," she
explained.

We didn't enter their area, since the reindeer were deep in
slumber. I hadn't caught a glimpse of one yet, but maybe there was
still a chance. Once evening rehearsals began, I might get lucky.
Just the possibility felt like it was enough for now.

A marble corridor opened into the administrative wing.

"Here we have staff offices, where scheduling, magic research,
event planning, and the occasional glitter explosion occur. And

just beyond that, we have our toy workshop, ReinDash hub, and the elf training wing, which you already got a peek of during the shuttle tour, so I won't be redundant."

She didn't waste any time. We continued down a side corridor, where the scent of herbs and something buttery drifted through the air. My nerves had dulled enough that hunger finally stirred in their place.

"On your right is our main restaurant with an exquisite, cozy setting, staffed by the finest chefs in the city. Feel free to stop by for lunch. It's a favorite among staff and guests alike."

With a playful flick of her wand, Gwenna indicated a set of doors lit with crystal sconces.

"Our bowling alley," she said with a grin. "Nikolas bowls… but I'm undefeated," she whispered.

We passed a gift shop, followed by a café and an indoor fountain.

The next area felt less like a workplace and more like a luxury retreat, with plush carpeting, amber lamplight flickering against gilded wallpaper, and the faint scent of cinnamon and clove lingering in the air.

"This is the West Wing," Gwenna said, gesturing down the corridor. "Private living quarters for our full-time staff. Nikolas lives in the North Wing, which is more secluded, of course, but still very much a part of everything. The rest of us are down this way. We don't tour the rooms, but the rumors of nightly gourmet chocolate sculptures at the bedside? All true. And delicious. The best turn-down service in town."

We continued on.

"Now, this," Gwenna said, lifting her wand in a graceful sweep toward the soaring arch lined with velvet drapes and golden statues, "is the Opera House. One of Nikolas's favorite spaces."

We stepped through the arch, which opened into a stunning two-story Opera House.

"We host full-scale productions here, including the annual Northpole Holiday Benefit Production."

Her gaze swept over the empty Opera House, then softened as it returned to me, gentle and reassuring.

"Jane, this is where you'll be spending most of your time. You'll be working in our professional opera theater, with state-of-the-art acoustics. Only the best make it on that stage."

I nodded, trying not to let it get to me—not the grandeur, not the expectation. Just take it one step at a time. I scanned the stage, the lights, the empty rows of velvet chairs, and took a slow breath, taking it all in.

Gwenna whisked me up to a balcony box seat, plush and private, with a view overlooking the Opera House. A glorious spread of my favorite dishes, from sweet to savory, waited for me—how they knew what I liked, I didn't know. But what I did know was that I could get used to this.

A crisp red welcome folder sat on the table, labeled "Jane Norwell, Performing Arts Instructor."

I took a seat and opened the folder, which included rehearsal schedules, a beautifully illustrated map of the estate, backstage notes, house guidelines, and an embossed program for the upcoming benefit, the title printed in embellished red script.

As a musical theater teacher, my job went far beyond choreography and teaching songs. I'd helped students find their voice, sometimes literally. I gave them a stage when they felt invisible, a script when they couldn't find the words, and applause when the world had only offered silence.

It wasn't easy. Rehearsals ran long. Budgets were tight. And there were days when even showing up felt like a small act of rebellion against burnout. But I believed in this with my whole heart. I believed that theater could change a kid's life. Maybe even save it.

I didn't teach for recognition. I taught because somewhere, deep down, I remembered what it felt like to be a kid with something to say and no place to say it.

The first half of orientation passed in a swirl of tinsel and surrealism. Gwenna's tour was thorough, but everything still felt larger than life.

She gave a few quick reminders as I gathered my folder, her voice echoing softly through the crimson-and-gold theater. I stood, ready to follow her to the next stop.

But something made me pause.

Below, the Opera House doors swung open. A measured bustle swept in with stagehands, assistants, a few performers. Rehearsal prep, maybe. Or a meeting. I wasn't sure.

Then I saw him.

A tall man in a striking red suit stepped onto the main floor, moving with an unspoken authority that seemed to bend the room around him.

Conversations hushed, as if the world held its breath, captivated by his presence.

He spoke little, nodding here and there, but every glance, every gesture carried weight. People leaned in, drawn to him not out of obligation, but instinct.

Even from here, there was something magnetic in the way he held himself, assured and in control without needing to prove it.

Platinum blond hair fell artfully across his face, a neatly kept beard, and features that made it hard to guess his age. Thirties? Forties? Whatever the number, he wore it well. And there was no denying it—he was handsome. Effortlessly so. Less jolly-old toymaker, more Northpole GQ.

Then, as if sensing my gaze, he turned slightly and looked up at me.

Our eyes locked. Time stood still. My heart skipped a beat, my fingers curled tighter around the edge of my folder. In his eyes, there was an undeniable spark—a flicker of intensity that sent a shiver down my spine. A quiet warmth lingered between us, electric and charged with an unspoken connection.

Then, with a final glance, he turned back to his team.

Nikolas.

I didn't speak his name aloud. I didn't have to. I felt it hum inside me, low and certain, like a spark igniting. Something stirred in me, something I couldn't explain. Suddenly, the stories, the mystery, the magic of his presence... all made sense.

I stepped into the hallway. Gwenna was already a few steps ahead.

There was still work to be done. But his gaze stayed with me, like the echo of a promise I didn't yet understand.

Chapter Six
A Tuesday in December

The rehearsal ended with the usual shuffle of goodbyes and reminders. Only this time, there was a little bit of magic in the air.

Our first session at the Palace had wrapped, and to my great delight, the kids were wonderful. A little chaotic and a little unsure, but eager. Being in the Palace rehearsal room brought a different kind of energy.

There were thirty in my sixth-grade class, each brimming with their own kind of charm (and unpredictability), a true reflection of their age—teetering between the last whispers of childhood and the first echoes of adolescence. Still enchanted by the magic of the stage, yet already bursting with opinions. And let me tell you, they had a lot to say!

We'd already spent a few weeks practicing at school, and by now, they had a solid grasp of their characters in our enchanting rendition of *The Twelve Days of Christmas*. I'd grouped them by verse, such as the turtle doves, the drummers, the ladies dancing, and of course, the coveted solo, the Partridge. A full festive ensemble, each group adding their own unique flair. Some numbers were packed with vibrant choreography, others leaned into vocals, and a few were still a little wobbly. But they were trying. They cared. And that alone made the show feel special.

The rehearsal room was smaller than the Opera House, but it still sparkled with marble columns, velvet curtains, and a row of mirrors that stretched across the wall like portals into another world.

Rehearsals were scheduled after school from 4:30 p.m. to 6:30 p.m. on weekdays, alternating between the studio and the main stage, with weekend mornings added to make the most of our limited time. Tomorrow, we'd be in the Opera House itself for their first time stepping onto a professional stage. I beamed at the thought as I stood at the front of the room, watching them scatter across the floor, their voices overlapping in bright, excited bursts.

A Palace guide arrived to escort the students down to the front gates, where their parents would pick them up. I made sure everyone was accounted for, then stepped back into the room. The space felt different now, quieter... softer. I only meant to stay ten, maybe fifteen minutes, just to put away the props and run through a few notes for tomorrow. But something about this place made it easy to stay. I felt good here. Focused. Home, even.

For a moment, I caught my reflection and laughed. My foot had turned out into fifth position without me even noticing. It had been years since I'd danced ballet, and even longer since I'd been in a real studio. At school, we made do with whatever space was available—classrooms, cafeterias, sometimes even hallways. But here, it felt like the floor remembered me. I'd always loved music and enjoyed singing, but dance was where it all began for me. It was my first language—my everything. Dance was where I felt the most like myself. I love teaching musical theater, but the choreography was always my favorite part of putting a show together. It wasn't just about counts and movements, but about the emotion behind them and the way a story could unfold without a single word. I let the stillness settle for a moment, then spun across the polished surface, ascending from a fourth position plié into a pirouette. Wobbly, sure, but still standing. I guess some things never really leave you.

Eventually, I packed up my things and made my way out. The Palace was still, in that dreamy way buildings get after hours. My footsteps echoed softly down the hall, past the golden lamplight of sconces and the hush of something magical still lingering in the air.

The night breeze was crisp against my cheeks, and snowflakes melted on my skin as I stepped out of the Palace, the final notes of rehearsal still humming in my bones.

But despite the rush and excitement of the evening, there was still no sign of a reindeer. No jingle of sleigh bells in the distance. And most of all, there was no Nikolas. Not that I was waiting for him. Not really. Still… every time the wind shifted or a door opened, I looked up. Just in case.

I adjusted my scarf and kept walking, one foot in front of the other, pretending the quiet didn't feel like disappointment. He was busy. Important. He had a whole Palace to manage. One moment of eye contact from a balcony didn't mean anything.

Except… it kind of did.

It stayed with me—the way he looked at me… and the way he looked. I tried to shake it off. I wasn't here for romance. I was here to do my job. But part of me, just a small, stubborn part, hoped I might see him again.

My phone vibrated in my pocket. I tugged off a glove to check it.

Celeste.

She was probably calling to check on me. I'd said I'd be home an hour ago, and instead I'd stayed behind, half-rehearsing, half-chasing some ghost of who I used to be.

I answered. "Hey."

"You didn't text, you didn't call—so either you got trapped in a storage closet… or you were having a candlelit dinner with the man in red. Please tell me it's the second one."

"Sorry to disappoint, but it definitely wasn't the second one. And sorry I didn't call. I just got caught up working on the routine. Lost track of time."

"So… did he at least show up?"

"No. Just the kids and a few stage managers."

"Hmm," she said in that tone that meant she was already drawing conclusions. "Maybe he's letting you settle in before he makes his next dramatic entrance."

"I'm not waiting for a dramatic entrance."

"You're not *not* waiting," she countered.

"Why would he come to my rehearsal anyway? It's not like we're the main performance. We're just the opening act."

"Give yourself some credit. How was it? Did your kids survive?"

"They did better than I expected. I think we might actually have a show by the end of this."

"See! Of course you will. You're good at this."

I didn't say anything. I just let her belief in me fill the silence.

"Well, I want to hear all about it," Celeste said. "I'll see you when you get home."

We ended the call just as I boarded the shuttle. My phone lit up again, this time with a text.

Dracula: "May I tempt you this evening?"

I stared at it for a second, then texted back, "Tempt me?"

Dracula: "A glass of wine in your hand. A story on the screen. Have you eaten yet?"

I couldn't help but grin as I texted back, "Not yet."

Dracula: "Then let me tempt you properly, with food, wine, and a movie. I'll take care of everything."

The simple offer touched me more than I expected. It felt nice to be thought of like that. Still, I took the shuttle ride and my drive home to think about it.

When I arrived home, Celeste was in the hallway outside Penny's room, holding a children's book and half-whispering warnings about "last chances" and "no more cookies." The nightlight was already on, and I could hear Penny bouncing around inside, still fully awake despite the bedtime hour. Celeste didn't notice me at first, too caught up in bedtime negotiations. She glanced over and mouthed "sorry" with a tired smile.

Celeste meant well. She always did. But between Penny's bedtime theatrics, Henry working late, and the general chaos of family life, we never really got the time together we said we would. Plans were made, then pushed back, then forgotten. And once Penny finally went down, I knew Celeste would too.

The guest room felt extra quiet. I sat alone in silence. The high from the Palace still unwavering—a tender ache of something unfinished in my chest. I wasn't ready for the night to end. I picked up my phone and hesitated, thumb hovering over Dracula's name. I didn't know if he was the one. But the holiday was getting closer. And I wasn't ready to give up hope, not yet. I still wanted to find someone.

It wasn't about dinner invites or bringing someone home for the holidays. It's not like I was going to drag a near-stranger to meet my family over mashed potatoes.

But still… I didn't want to walk into another Christmas wondering if I'd missed my shot at something real. I wanted to feel hopeful that love was still possible. That somewhere out there, someone would be thinking of me that day. Someone I could text Merry Christmas to… and who'd actually mean it when they said it back. I just wanted to feel like I was finally moving toward something, toward someone.

I opened Messages and texted Dracula, "Yes."

Dracula's apartment? Straight out of a Gothic home magazine. Dark walls, brocade fabrics, and antique mirrors were everywhere, an absurd number of them, really, for someone without a reflection.

There was a single dinner plate set at the table for me. He poured me a glass of red wine. Then poured himself something darker. Definitely not wine.

It was already late when I got there, so I figured he'd order takeout or something simple. But no. The food was good—weirdly good, especially for someone I assumed didn't cook. Steak, beets, sautéed spinach. Dark chocolate for dessert.

"This is amazing," I said, genuinely impressed.

His lips curved, hungry with unspoken intent. "It's iron-rich and good for the body. Keeps the blood sweet… vibrant."

I laughed. He didn't.

I kept eating. He didn't touch a thing. He just sat there, swirling his drink, watching me with an indulgent fascination, like I was the most interesting episode of a guilty pleasure TV show—predictable, maybe, but completely addicting.

After dinner, we moved to the couch. Lights dim. Movie queued up—some overly moody black-and-white film with tragic violin music. I settled in with my wine. We hadn't even hit the opening credits when I felt him inching closer.

Then a hand brushed my shoulder. His cold fingers traced the line of my neck.

"You're warm," he murmured. "I like that."

"Thanks?" I scooted half an inch away.

He leaned in again. "I can hear it."

"Hear what?" I asked.

"Your blood," he whispered. "It sings."

Okay, and there it was.

I set my wine down. "Are you trying to drink my blood on the first date?"

He leaned back into the couch, a smug grin playing on his lips. "I'm just… savoring the moment."

"Yeah, well, the moment's over." I stood. "This isn't what I thought you meant by dinner and a movie."

He raised an eyebrow. "Then what did you think it meant?"

"Exactly what you said. Dinner and a movie."

"We are watching a movie," he said, his eyes never leaving my neck.

That was the moment I knew.

He didn't want to date me.

He wanted to drink me.

"Just a taste," he murmured, tilting his head.

"I should go."

He didn't argue. He just smiled. Like he knew I'd be back. Like no one ever said no for long.

The next morning, I sipped coffee in the kitchen while Penny hummed into her cereal and Celeste packed her lunch, sneaking glances at me like she had something on her mind.

A piece of bacon slipped off my plate and hit the floor. Princess Butterscotch made her move like she'd been training for this moment her whole life, then plopped back under the table, keeping guard for the next drop.

"Where'd you disappear to last night?" Celeste asked finally.

I groaned. "Dracula's. For what I thought would be dinner and a movie, but turned out to be more of a bloodlust call."

Celeste smirked. "Let me guess—he invited you over to 'watch something'?"

"Yep."

She shook her head. "Jane. That's code."

"I figured that out when he tried to tongue my artery."

Penny looked up. "What's code?"

"Nothing," we said at the same time.

I left for work, slightly traumatized, marginally flattered, and extremely caffeinated. At least the week could only go up from here. I put on my favorite playlist, drummed my fingers on the steering wheel, and told myself it was going to be a good day.

It had to be.

Chapter Seven
Garland

Welp, I was wrong. Today wasn't a good day.

I walked out the door this morning feeling hopeful—good playlist, good coffee, good vibes. By mid-morning though, the universe had other plans. I'd found out my lead vocalist was getting whisked off to Arizona for winter break by her snowbird parents and wouldn't be able to do the performance. The show was hanging by a thread. So, of course, my mind couldn't help jumping to the other things hanging by a thread too—like my love life. With Christmas right around the corner, I had a sinking feeling I wouldn't find anyone in time. And just to top it off, my car was hanging by a thread too. It wouldn't start.

I tried twice and then a third time, just in case, but all I got was a weak sputter before it gave up completely. The dashboard lights flickered, but the engine didn't even try. Battery? Starter? I didn't know. I just knew it wasn't budging.

I slumped back into the driver's seat, phone in hand, already dreading the conversation. I hated relying on people. Even Celeste. She already had enough on her plate, and she and Henry were nice enough to let me stay at their place while I figured out my next steps.

"Hey," I said into the phone. "Are you still picking up Penny from her art thing today?"

"Yeah, just got her," Celeste said. "Why?"

"My car won't start. Again… Can you swing by and work your magic or something? The kids already left on the shuttle, and I'm supposed to be at rehearsal in thirty minutes."

She sighed. "You and that car… yeah, we're five minutes away."

A few minutes later, Celeste's car pulled into the school lot. Penny was in the backseat, chattering about the letter of the day and show-and-tell. Celeste stepped out, gave a theatrical flick of her wrist, and muttered something under her breath. I turned the key. Nothing. Not even a click.

She tried again. Still nothing.

Celeste winced. "If it were something simple, like the battery, it would've worked. But cars have too many moving parts."

"No worries," I said, removing the keys. "I know your magic can only do so much. Thanks for trying."

"You're going to need a mechanic. Come on, hop in. I'll give you a ride."

Celeste's car rolled to a stop just outside the Palace's staff gate with ten minutes to spare. Hopefully I wouldn't be late after all.

I was halfway out the door when Penny pressed her face to the window.

"Aunt Jane, can I come with you? Please? I wanna see the Palace!"

Celeste rolled down the window, and I leaned in toward Penny. "Sweetheart, you need a special pass to go inside. You'll get to see everything at the benefit show, I promise."

She pouted dramatically. "But that's forever from now."

Before I could respond, a Palace elf in a mossy green uniform popped up beside the car, holding a small glowing badge.

"She wants to come in?" he asked, already handing the pass through the window.

I blinked. "Wait—what?"

With a twinkle in his eye, he said, "Anything for Jane."

I stared at him. "Seriously?"

The elf just winked and tipped his cap before vanishing behind the gate as if he'd never been there.

The badge twinkled in Penny's hands. She squealed, jumped out of the car, and threw her arms around me.

"She's all yours," Celeste said. "I've got errands to run, and she's been begging to see this place for days. Win-win."

Celeste drove off faster than either of us could say goodbye. I guess even magical sisters need a babysitter every now and then.

Penny clutched her pass like it was a golden ticket and bounced down the hall beside me.

I made it to rehearsal with a few minutes to spare and got Penny settled in a front-row seat. She sat there smiling from ear to ear, swinging her legs and watching like she was at a Broadway show.

I clapped my hands to bring everyone into formation. It was only our second rehearsal at the Palace, and our first time on the main stage. I just hoped they could handle it.

We had barely begun vocal warm-ups when a figure appeared at the back of the Opera House, cloaked in an air of mystery and refinement. He wore a long, tailored black coat, with crisply pressed trousers and a white shirt fastened by a stiff, high collar.

A white scarf was knotted at his throat, and over it all, a billowing black cloak swept behind him like a shadow.

And then there was his face. Or half of it. Even from a distance, I could see the paint—white and bone-like, shaped in the image of a skull, covering one side like he was hiding something. He didn't introduce himself. His expression never shifted. He just hovered, then drifted down the center aisle like he was judging a competition I never entered. He stepped closer, approaching the stage as if I'd invited him up, even though I hadn't.

Up close, the paint was even more intricate than I'd realized. A stylized skeleton in ivory and charcoal, with black accents hollowing the eye socket and tracing the bone-sharp edge of his cheek, like something sacred and ceremonial. The other half of his face remained bare. Pale, sharp, and impossibly stern. Everything about him teetered just shy of theatrical. And his expression? The kind that suggested he disapproved of everything—including the air.

He watched for a solid five minutes, then finally cut through the stage lights with a sharp, "What is this?"

I blinked. "Sorry?"

He pointed at the students, two of whom had just launched into an off-key harmony while pretending to be French hens. "What is this?"

"A rehearsal," I said.

"For what, exactly?"

"The benefit production. We're the school district showcase."

His brow furrowed. "You're not supposed to be on the main stage today. The Opera Company has this slot."

I paused. "No—we were cleared for Wednesdays, Fridays, and weekend mornings."

He frowned and whipped out his cell phone, scrolling furiously. "They said Tuesdays and Thursdays."

I was already pulling up my email. "No, here—Wednesdays, Fridays, and weekend mornings. I triple-confirmed with scheduling."

He glanced at it, then let out a tight breath, somewhere between resignation and irritation. "They've changed it again."

"Seems like it," I muttered, trying not to roll my eyes.

I waited for him to walk away, but he stayed, watching as the kids broke into a shaky run-through of the opening number. Their entrances were a little off, and two of my strongest singers forgot their lyrics and tried to improvise in rhyme. I laughed and clapped anyway, partly to lift their spirits, partly to cover my own flubbed cue, not to mention that one awful note I cracked earlier, still echoing in my head. We were all a little off today, and I couldn't even blame them. Losing our soloist at the last minute had thrown everyone. But they were still here, still trying. That mattered more than pitch.

The man in the cloak didn't seem to agree. He watched it all with a face like he'd bitten into a lemon.

I cleared my throat. "Is there something else?"

"No," he said. "It's… charming."

He said it like "charming" was code for "please make it stop." I bit my tongue and took a slow breath, aware of Penny watching. The last thing I needed was to lose my cool in front of the kids, especially with Penny already giving him the kind of squinty glare that meant she was mentally flipping through her spellbook. I turned my focus back to the group, pretending not to notice him still watching.

After a few more minutes, the man in the cloak turned on his heel and disappeared through a side door, stage left.

When rehearsal ended and the kids were dismissed, I stayed behind to gather our things. Penny twirled in the center aisle, mouthing the words to *The Twelve Days of Christmas* under her breath. I caught her eye and gave her a wink. She grinned and wiggled in place, attempting her own version of the nine ladies dancing.

We hadn't used many props today, just a few crowns and some toy flutes, so cleanup was quick. A few minutes later, we made our way out a side hallway, where the corridor glittered with gold tinsel and peppermint-scented garland.

Penny's eyes went wide.

The corridor ahead had been transformed into a life-sized winter village. Snow dusted the floor in a glittering layer of white, edged by marshmallow snowbanks, and gumdrops the size of basketballs. Towering gingerbread houses lined the path, each one frosted with swirls of icing and crowned with peppermint shingles. Candy canes towered like lampposts, standing at attention beside sugar plum trees and licorice fences.

Penny let out a delighted gasp and skipped a few steps ahead of me. A toy train chugged through one of the snowy yards, its tracks weaving between a family of cheerful snowmen in scarves. One of them waved.

As we wandered past an ice-carved ballerina and a towering Nutcracker, Penny pointed toward a figure up ahead. "Look! It's Santa!" she beamed, her voice bubbling with excitement.

I stepped closer.

A life-size statue stood beneath a soft spotlight, sculpted from what looked like crystal or enchanted ice. It was incredibly detailed, capturing a figure layered for winter in a regal, sweeping coat. His hair was windswept, and his expression calm with a hint of a smile beneath steadfast devotion.

It was him.

Nikolas.

That fleeting moment on the balcony flashed back—platinum hair falling across his face, his confident stance, and eyes that held a smoldering intensity I hadn't been able to forget.

My chest tightened.

I hadn't seen him again since, yet he stayed on my mind. I tried not to think about him. He probably didn't even remember me. Still, I couldn't stop wondering if he did.

Up ahead, Penny had already skipped several steps farther, pulled in by the beauty of it all, and I felt it too. The hall around us glimmered as if we'd stepped straight into a snow globe.

We followed the peppermint-striped path to the end of the corridor and into the elevator bay. I pressed the button and pulled out my phone to check the time. Celeste wasn't due for a few more minutes. A new text from her was waiting on my screen.

Celeste: "Leaving now. Be there in twenty."

I started to tuck my phone away, but another text slid in.

Dracula: "Did you leave something behind at my place... a glass slipper?"

I blinked, thinking, *Glass slipper?* "Wrong girl," I replied.

Dracula: "No, I remember now. You left an impression I couldn't shake."

"Then what's my name?" I texted back.

Dracula: "Something far too beautiful to be contained in a word."

Me: "So... you don't even know who you're texting? We literally had dinner last night."

Dracula: "Why must you deny me so?"

I shook my head, smirking despite myself, and slid my phone back into my pocket. That's when I noticed Penny wasn't at my side anymore.

I turned a slow circle. She was just here.

A burst of giggles echoed from down the hall. Of course.

I followed the sound and found her standing near a set of gleaming, oversized doors with reindeer silhouettes carved in silver above the archway. I jogged to catch up.

"We can't go in there."

Penny's hand was already on the handle. She slipped inside without hesitation, and I followed before the door could swing shut behind her.

"Penny," I started, instinctively reaching for her.

I meant to say something about boundaries. About rules. About how we probably weren't allowed in here without a guide. But I couldn't bring myself to break the moment.

The space beyond was quiet and dimly lit, the air cool and fragrant with pine and something sweeter, like hay dusted in cinnamon and sugar. Lanterns hung from vaulted beams above, spilling a soft, silvery light across the straw-lined floor.

At the far end, through a series of arched exits, the outdoors opened wide with snow blanketing the courtyard beneath a navy sky, speckled with stars. A low mist drifted along the ground, swirling faintly in the moonlight.

At first, I didn't see them. Then a soft snort echoed from one of the stalls.

A pair of eyes blinked at me.

Then another. And another.

Suddenly, they were all there, emerging from the misty shadows with slow, elegant steps, their hooves whispering against the straw. They took formation in a loose crescent, flanking the center aisle with absolute splendor.

"Reindeer," Penny gasped.

Eight of them stood before us, proud and regal, with antlers branching wide like winter oak trees. Their rich chestnut coats were brightened by soft cream fur along their chests and necks. Together, they radiated a quiet strength and benevolence.

Penny inched closer, her face alight with fascination. The reindeer held still and calm, simply acknowledging our presence from across the stable.

"They're so pretty," Penny said in awe.

They were more than pretty. They were breathtaking—each one a living sculpture of power and brilliance, as if the forest and the snow and every ancient thing had come together to create them. Their eyes were beautiful and magnificent, holding something old, something knowing.

I touched Penny's shoulder lightly. "Come on," I whispered. "We shouldn't be in here."

She sighed, casting one last glance over her shoulder as we turned toward the door.

"Going so soon?"

A voice broke the silence.

We froze.

I turned, slowly. No one stood there. Just the reindeer. They hadn't moved. Or maybe they had—I couldn't tell. Then the one in the center, tall with a chestnut coat that caught hints of silver in the light, tilted her head, watching me with curiosity.

Penny tugged at my sleeve. "Did you hear that too?"

The center reindeer stepped forward.

"You've already woken us," she said—her voice even, her expression unchanged. But somehow, I knew the words had come from her.

Their mouths didn't move. But somehow, I could hear them—clear and calm, as if the words formed in my chest instead of my ears. Gentle, resonant, and impossible to ignore.

The reindeer were a rare sight, and as far as anyone knew, they never spoke. Yet here they were, addressing us like it was the most natural thing in the world.

Penny's eyes went wide. "They talk."

"It appears so," I murmured, still steadying myself on the strangeness of hearing their voices.

"I'm sorry we woke you," I said quickly. "We didn't mean to—I didn't think the door would be open."

"It's fine. We were waking anyway. And if you happen to have a candy cane... all the better."

"I'm afraid I don't have—"

Before I could finish, Penny was already digging deep in her coat pocket and pulling out a single red-and-white candy cane.

I muttered something about not feeding them, which went in one ear and out the other as Penny stepped closer and held out the candy cane like an offering. The reindeer lowered her head and began nibbling the red-and-white swirl right from Penny's palm.

Penny giggled with wonder as the reindeer's whiskers tickled her skin. With a final crunch of peppermint, she finished the treat, licking her lips, pleased. "A touch of peppermint goes a long way after a deep slumber."

Then, to our astonishment, she bent one knee and said, "Climb on, little one. You've earned yourself a ride on the Dancer Express."

Penny beamed, and I blinked in recognition. The reindeer's poised posture, her delicate steps, the dancer-like ease of her movements—Dancer. Of course. Yes.

Penny glanced up at me, wide-eyed. "Can I?"

I hesitated, but only for a moment.

No one had told us we couldn't be here. But no one had exactly invited us in, either. Rehearsal was over. The lights were low. I hadn't meant to linger this long. Still… how could I deny her this? The wonder in Penny's eyes, the magic thick in the air—I was caught in it too. Whatever this was, it felt right. The moment was too perfect to ruin.

I nodded.

She climbed onto Dancer's back with care, slipping her boots into the small stirrups of the saddle and gripping the pommel for balance. She adjusted her seat, steadying herself.

Dancer rose beneath her, then stepped forward in slow, measured strides down the center path, with me walking alongside. As we passed, the reindeer stirred in quiet acknowledgment.

To the left, one gave a short burst of movement, trotting in a small arc before settling back into place, like she was just warming up.

"Dasher," Dancer murmured. "Still thinks everything's a race."

To the right, another pawed precisely at the ground in a perfect four-count, every step sharp, and a little theatrical.

"Prancer," Dancer said with a nod. "Always performing."

A third reindeer lifted her head with slow elegance, then gave a soft, amused snort—like she knew she was being admired.

"That's Vixen," Dancer said, a hint of fondness in her voice.

The others dipped their heads in silent recognition.

"Comet. Cupid. Donner. Blitzen," Dancer said. Their names settled in the air like stars being counted aloud.

Penny straightened in the saddle. "I'm Penny," she said proudly.

I opened my mouth to introduce myself, but a voice carried from beyond the archway at the far end of the courtyard.

"We know who you are."

A glow began to rise through the mist, illuminating the scene like the first light of dawn.

Then she appeared. With antlers glowing and graceful hooves barely stirring the snow, a majestic reindeer stepped forward. Her coat was chestnut and cream like the others, but her antlers shimmered with an ethereal glow, smooth and white-gold like crystal branches lit from within.

The other reindeer parted for her without a sound, honoring her presence. She stepped into full view, larger, wiser, and serene as moonlight cascading over the landscape.

The glowing reindeer paused before us. Her gaze met mine, and in that moment, something passed between us—subtle but unmistakable. She was absolutely beautiful, leaving me speechless and full of amazement.

Who was she? And how did she know who I was?

Her voice came soft and sure. "Yes, Jane Norwell. And Penny Everhart."

I hadn't asked her aloud, but she responded, tilting her head like she'd heard me anyway.

I brushed it off. Surely she read it from my name badge.

Her eyes glimmered with amusement. "Your names were not read from the badges you wear."

Her words echoed the very thought I'd just formed. I blinked, stunned. She heard that?

She turned her antlers slightly, casting a golden halo across the straw. "Knowledge runs through us like starlight through the heavens. We know the skies, and we know pure hearts. Your thoughts are gentle echoes. We hear what is given freely."

For a moment, we just stood there, taking her in—this noble presence who somehow felt like both a stranger and someone we'd always known.

Then Penny asked, "What's your name?"

"Garland," the reindeer replied, her eyes glinting with warmth, as if smiling.

She offered no title, no explanation, just a name. But the way the others had parted for her, silent, instinctive, almost sacred, said everything. She wasn't just one of them. She was the matriarch.

Penny's eyes were wide. "It's nice to meet you, Garland."

"The pleasure is ours," Garland replied, her voice warm and resonant. She began to step back, but Penny's heartfelt plea gave her pause. "Can we stay with you?" she asked suddenly. "Just a little longer?"

Garland's eyes twinkled with understanding. "That would be nice," she said softly. "But your mother just arrived."

I blinked. A second later, my phone chimed in my pocket. I pulled it out. A new text appeared on my screen.

Celeste: "I'm outside. Ready when you are."

"Our paths will cross again soon," Garland said, her voice carrying certainty.

I helped Penny down from Dancer's back. She landed gently beside me, still wide-eyed.

I looked up again, but Garland was already walking away, her form growing fainter as the mist drifted in around her. One by one, the others followed. And then they were gone.

Later that night, I lay in bed with the covers pulled to my chin. Penny had fallen asleep grinning, whispering something about "Garland the Glowing Reindeer" just before drifting off.

I was happy she'd been there, sharing the wonder with me. Even in a world full of magic, something about our time with the reindeer felt different.

I pulled the covers tighter around me and turned off the lights. But the glow of Garland's antlers still shone in my mind.

She was a beautiful sight. But maybe what moved me most was the feeling I had every time I stepped through those Palace gates—like anything was possible.

I'd started the day with the news that my lead soloist was leaving me solo-less for the big night, then wound up with a broken-down car, and capped it off with some mysterious man in a cloak criticizing my work.

It hadn't exactly been a winning streak. I'd woken up still disappointed from last night's date and silently wondering if I'd ever find the kind of connection I was hoping for before Christmas. But somehow, by the end of it all... today had turned into one of the most beautiful days—one I knew I'd remember for a long time. Not because everything went right, but because something unexpected and something extraordinary had found me anyway.

Chapter Eight
The Duet

The line at the Palace coffee shop was moving slower than a dress rehearsal with a sprained ankle. I checked the time again. Rehearsal started in ten minutes, and I still had three people ahead of me. Today's rehearsal was going to be hectic. I still didn't have a replacement for my lead soloist and would be holding auditions for the spot. I needed caffeine. Desperately.

I stepped slightly out of line and craned my neck to see what the holdup was. That's when I saw him.

Of course. Not Nikolas. That would've been too convenient. You never run into the people you want to see. No—fate, ever petty, delivered the man in the cloak, in full brooding composer mode, holding up the line, probably asking if the espresso notes were in D minor.

I hadn't seen him since he barged into my rehearsal yesterday, cloak flaring and voice sharp, accusing me of hijacking the stage. As if I didn't know where I was supposed to be, didn't know how to run a rehearsal, didn't know how to do my job. He never said those exact words, but the message was clear enough—I didn't belong there.

I looked at my watch. Apparently, I didn't belong in this line, either. Not if I planned to start rehearsal on time.

I turned, ready to flee before—

"Jane."

Too late. How does he even know my name?

I turned back slowly, forcing a polite smile. "Oh. Hi."

He stepped closer, catching up to me with a latte in hand. "I was… less than kind yesterday," he said. "I wanted to apologize and introduce myself properly."

"I'm Phantom."

"I'm Jane. But it seems like you already knew that."

His expression tilted sheepish. "I asked someone on the Palace staff. But I should've taken the time to ask you yesterday."

He gestured toward the counter. "I'd like to make it up to you. Let me buy your coffee?"

I hesitated. Then again, I really did need the coffee.

"Please," he added. "Whatever your heart desires."

I relented. "Okay… thank you. I've been craving a peppermint mocha all day."

He paid for my drink and, surprisingly, walked with me to the rehearsal wing. Turns out he knew a shortcut. Today we were in the studio, not the main stage. I made it on time… and maybe even in a better mood.

We didn't talk much, but it wasn't awkward. It was almost… charming? And if I wasn't mistaken, he was flirting with me. He dropped me off and said he enjoyed our time. As he walked away, I watched him disappear down the corridor, his cloak trailing behind him like a closing curtain.

Maybe he wasn't so bad after all.

I stood alone in the studio going over choreography. Rehearsal went better than expected. The group was finally starting to get used to the larger space and feeling more confident in their formations. And much to my relief, I'd found a replacement for the Partridge solo—one of the girls from chorus who stepped up like it was no big deal.

But it was a big deal.

This wasn't just another school recital. It was the benefit, the biggest holiday event of the year. The most-watched broadcast in the country. And she jumped in with confidence. Excitement. Bravery. I couldn't help but be moved, watching her. There was a time I'd felt that way too. But that felt like forever ago.

I drew in a breath and did a few pas de bourrées, maybe searching for that confidence again. I wasn't sure. But a soft knock at the rehearsal room door made me pause mid-step.

I opened the door, glancing each way down the long corridors—no one was there. On the floor, just inside the threshold, lay a pristine white envelope. I bent to pick it up. It was thick, heavy, expensive-looking. Sealed with a dark wax stamp, a symbol I didn't recognize pressed into the center. My name was inked across the front in impossibly ornate handwriting.

Inside, there was a single card, thick and ivory-toned, with a riddle written across the center in looping black ink.

The heart holds chambers, deep and true,
With mirrored walls reflecting you.
The way begins not with the known,
But with what's felt—by heart alone.
—Phantom

I just stood there, staring at the words. Then, before I even realized it, I placed my hand over my heart. *Follow not what is known but what's felt by heart...* Follow my heart?

The meaning was already there, the thought still forming as I said it to myself. The heart has chambers. Four, right? *Chambers that are deep and true, with mirrored walls...* Reflecting me?

My eyes lifted to the row of mirrors across the studio. I walked past each one, murmuring the numbers—one, two, three, four.

There was something different about the fourth. Not obvious. Not right away. Only if you looked close enough. Or maybe... I was just following my heart.

As I stepped closer, I noticed it—the faintest draft brushing past my legs. A narrow gap between the frame and the wall. Subtle things, but enough to set it apart.

I placed both hands firmly against the cool glass. I leaned in with certainty and pressed forward. A click sounded, and the mirror slowly gave way, swinging open to reveal a hidden entrance. A secret passage.

Behind it lay a narrow hallway, candlelit, with a trail of rose petals scattered across the floor. A quiet gasp escaped my lips as I gazed at the beauty of it. The note slipped from my hand, forgotten, as I stepped inside.

The candles flickered as I passed, lighting the path ahead. The air smelled faintly of wax and roses. At the far end of the corridor, Phantom stood waiting for me. He stepped forward slowly, holding a single red rose. When I reached him, he held it out gently, like an offering, and I accepted. He extended his hand again, silent and assured. I slipped my hand into his, and his fingers curled around mine, like it was a cue he'd been waiting for.

Together, we walked through a series of hushed passageways— past framed oil portraits, racks of forgotten costumes, and staircases leading to places I couldn't see. We took one of them, following the spiral upward until we reached a door. Phantom turned the knob, and the door opened to a narrow, dim corridor tucked behind the balcony level of the Opera House.

He led me to a box seat, dimly lit, with a table set for two already waiting. Candlelight flickered over silverware and crystal, the setting beautifully arranged and nestled in the shadowed curve of the balcony. Below us, the Opera House stretched out in golden silence, all plush red velvet and gilded scrollwork, empty and ours alone.

He pulled out my chair. And for a while, we simply ate quietly and peacefully, the way people do when something's simmering beneath the surface but neither one wants to be the first to stir it.

"This is absolutely beautiful," I said finally. "The dinner. The Opera House."

He looked out over the empty theater, his voice low. "I wasn't always welcome in rooms like this. I was born… different. People saw my face before they ever saw me."

I hesitated, unsure what to say. But I knew what it felt like to be on the outside, and his sudden warmth loosened my defenses just enough to let the words slip out.

"I get that." I finally confessed. "Maybe not the face part. But the different part. Everyone around me seems so special, so magical. And I'm just… well, I don't know what I am."

"It's not a bad thing, you know—being different. Just lonely sometimes."

"That's the part I know best."

"Loneliness?"

I nodded, the admission both painful and strangely comforting.

"It helps if you have a release. What makes you happy, Jane?"

"I'd say… dance, choreography, movement. They make me happy. That's how I connect."

He didn't dismiss it, but his voice grew more fervent.

"Movement is powerful, yes. But music is the language beneath it all. A melody can travel from one city to the next, from country to country—no translation needed. It unites people who've never met. Helps us feel. Helps us hear what we've buried. That's why I sing. That's why I'm here."

I hesitated. He made it sound so meaningful, so effortless. I'd never been good at expressing myself, not like that. Words always felt clumsy in my mouth, like I couldn't shape them fast enough to match what I felt. In rooms full of people, I faded. I didn't shine. I didn't sparkle. I just… existed. I was different, sure, but not the kind that drew attention. Just the kind that kept you on the outside of everything.

His eyes found mine.

"Let's find your voice, Jane. Sing with me."

My stomach tightened. He made it sound so easy, like singing was something sacred, something waiting inside me to be released. But it wasn't that simple. I could sing in front of children, sure, in classrooms, on cozy stages with paper backdrops and forgiving faces. But this? This wasn't a school performance. This was a man who lived for music, who spoke about melody like it was breath and survival. And now he was looking at me like he expected something more.

I knew I could carry a tune. I wasn't bad. But I wasn't anything special. I was just a teacher—someone who used to dream a little bigger, before life taught me not to.

I glanced at the stage below, then back at him. He looked back at me.

"I heard you during rehearsal," he said with measured poise. "You have a voice. A beautiful one. You just need the right partner."

I hesitated. "You mean teacher?"

That's what they always said. I had potential. I had heart. I just needed the right training, the right support, the right teacher. Funny, considering I was one. But they didn't mean the kind who taught musical theater to sixth graders or coached stage fright out of nervous middle schoolers. They meant the kind with clients on world tours and conservatory résumés. The kind who turned raw talent into legends and standing ovations.

Well, I'd had all of it. Lessons. Practice. Workshops. Years of trying to be good enough. This was as good as it got.

Phantom met my eyes across the candlelight, his voice carrying a soft resolve.

"Sing with me."

Maybe I hadn't given up on singing completely… but I'd learned how to live with the dull ache of disappointment. How to tuck it into the background and focus on the things I was good at. Because I was good at something. Teaching. I knew how to reach a classroom, how to connect with the shy kid in the back row, how to pull a performance out of a group of sixth-graders who'd never been on stage before. That had to count for something. It had to mean something. Because if everything I've given to my students, to this job, to making peace with letting go wasn't enough… then I wasn't sure what else I had left to give.

Phantom looked at me like the answer was simple. Like all I had to do… was sing. Then he stood humming a single note, deep and unbroken. He extended his hand to me.

For a moment, I just stared at it, hesitating and uncertain. Then I reached for him. His fingers wrapped gently around mine, as he led me out of the box into the winding passageways.

He began to sing as we walked, his voice low and intimate, like a confession meant only for me. The melody rose slowly, swelling in the air as he sang:

I am the shadow, I am the light.
Misunderstood, but maybe not tonight.
Will you take my hand, will you keep my secrets?
I'll show you things you did not know existed.

As the final note floated between us, he turned to me, open and inviting.

A look.

A question.

A cue.

And something in me stirred, pulling me into the moment and I sang:

I am no shadow, but I'm no light.
Invisible, most of my life.
But something special's happening in this place.
I'll take your hand. Show me the way.

We drifted through the quiet corridors. No crowds. Just the music—his voice guiding us forward.

We moved in rhythm through velvet-curtained halls and shadowed stairwells, until the passageway opened into the wings of the grand stage.

We stepped onto center stage. The curtains were already drawn. The theater before us was vast and hushed, bathed in the resplendence of the chandelier. Rows of empty velvet seats stretched out like stars in a still sky.

For a moment, we just stood there in the spotlight, singing a song that had never existed until now. Two silhouettes. One song. And it belonged to us.

We finished the duet, the final notes echoing up into the domed ceiling like applause.

Silence fell between us. He stepped closer.

"You don't need a spotlight to be seen, Jane. You only need to stop hiding."

I met his gaze, kindness in my eyes as my words carried a delicate truth.

"Says the man hiding behind the mask."

He smiled knowingly, then took my hand, pressing a light kiss to the back of it. "It's been lovely," he said. "Until we meet again tomorrow."

Then, as if the scene were done, he turned and disappeared into the shadows of the wings—leaving me standing alone at center stage.

Chapter Nine
Under the Stars

Saturday, 2:04 a.m.
New text message:
Dracula: "Still thinking about you, enchantress."
2:06 a.m.
Dracula: "That night left its mark on me. Did I leave one on you?" 😉
2:09 a.m.
Dracula: "Indulge me. One pic. Neck only."
2:10 a.m.
Dracula: "Just a taste?"

I didn't answer. I stared at the screen for a second, then turned it face down on the nightstand. My mind wasn't on Dracula. It was Phantom I kept waiting for.

I hadn't heard a word from him. No cryptic notes. No calls. Not even a text. Not that I expected one, not at this hour. But still, Friday had come and gone, and with it, all the anticipation I didn't want to admit I'd been holding onto.

By the time our mid-morning rehearsal rolled around, I'd done what I always do—thrown myself into the work. And it paid off. Rehearsal in the Opera House had gone well and was right on track. The kids stayed focused, the cues landed, and energy stayed up through the final number. With only two rehearsals left until showtime, I was feeling cautiously optimistic.

I started gathering my things, ready to head out. My bag was halfway over my shoulder when I heard the stage doors swing open.

The Snow Bridge Ballet swept in like a gust of velvet and tulle, their directors trailing behind them with headsets and coffee. Someone called out for spacing. Someone else adjusted the lights. It was organized chaos in pointe shoes.

I stepped aside to let them pass, but didn't quite make it to the door. Instead, I drifted to a seat in the back row of the velvet house and let myself get pulled in.

They were rehearsing *The Nutcracker*, my favorite. A holiday tradition since I was a child. A ritual, really. I used to watch it every December with my mom, curled up on the couch with cinnamon popcorn and fuzzy socks. Later, I danced in it—first as a mouse, then a Marzipan, and eventually, for one glorious winter, as the Sugar Plum Fairy.

It had been years since I'd seen it. Longer since I'd let myself feel it. But sitting there in the shadowed rows, I sank right back into the magic.

The Christmas Eve party filled the stage with twinkling lights and swirling skirts. Clara received her Nutcracker, and the world shifted. The battle with the Mouse King was bold and chaotic. The transformation was sudden, sweeping, just like I remembered.

Snowflakes danced across the stage with perfect precision, flurrying into the Land of Sweets. The colors deepened, the music swelled, and each variation brought something new—Spanish, Arabian, Chinese, Russian.

Then came the Sugar Plum Fairy. Her Pas de Deux was so light, so impossibly delicate, it made my throat ache. I remembered every step of it, every lift, every turn, and every moment I used to dream about.

And when Clara awoke from it all, unsure if it had ever really happened, I felt that too. Because maybe that's the most magical part of the ballet—the way it lingers like a dream you don't want to wake up from.

I stayed in my seat a little longer than I meant to, letting the music fade and the lights come back up.

Dancers trickled out. Crew came in. The atmosphere shifted, with crisp tutus and falling snow giving way to dark velvet and rising fog. A few cast members emerged in fragments of costume—icefiligree crowns, silver masks, iridescent cloaks that glimmered like midnight ice.

This wasn't some middle school musical. This was Phantom's world.

The cast of *Nocturne of Winter's Opera* had been rehearsing for weeks now, but I hadn't seen a glimpse until today. Now, from the same seat I'd watched *The Nutcracker*, I found myself watching again. Just for a minute. Maybe five. Maybe more.

The performance was breathtaking. Every note, every movement landed exactly where it should. It was flawless, so precise it hardly felt real. And yet, it still wasn't enough. Not for him.

Everything stopped. A hush fell over the stage like someone had cut the air. He stepped out of the shadows.

Phantom.

He was unrushed and unapologetic, every inch of him composed. His black cloak brushed the floor as his eyes scanned the cast like a conductor preparing a storm.

"I'm making some changes," he said, his voice precise and clear, slicing through the silence.

No one moved.

He walked to center stage. "Don't worry, you're all doing... fine." He tilted his head slightly. "But fine isn't art. It's not what this world needs."

He flicked his hand toward the wings.

"I've found someone who will elevate this performance. Someone who understands what it means to haunt an aria."

I leaned forward, my heart sinking before I even knew why.

She glided in like an angel, luminous in a gown of starlight and spun silk. She moved across the stage without sound and without effort.

"This," Phantom said, gesturing to her as if unveiling a masterpiece, "is Miss Christine Daaé, the newest addition to our final act."

A ripple of gasps and murmurs passed through the cast. One of the performers—Queen of the Northern Star, maybe—stepped forward like she meant to protest. Phantom lifted a single finger.

Silence.

"We'll adjust," he said. "That's what artists do."

The cast looked stunned. A few nodded stiffly while most didn't move.

I stayed frozen in my seat as Christine took her mark and began to sing.

And then I understood. It wasn't just that she could sing. It was the way she filled the space, as if the theater itself was breathing with her. Every note poured out in crystal tones, unshakable and commanding.

He watched her the whole time, his eyes fixed. It was the kind of look people spend their whole lives hoping to earn, as if she was the meaning of everything. I knew that look. I'd seen it once when he looked at me. And now I knew what it had meant.

But he hadn't wanted me. Not really. He'd wanted a muse. And when I hadn't risen to meet that role, when I'd faltered, flinched, second-guessed, he found someone who didn't.

Someone extraordinary.

I sank back slowly in my seat, suddenly colder than I'd been all evening. So that's what he meant when he said it was okay to be different. Turns out he meant different like her—dazzling, operatic, spotlight-ready. Not me. Not some middle school talent show teacher.

The rehearsal wrapped up not long after. I stayed behind in my seat, pretending to check messages I didn't have. Part of me was sure he'd seen me. Phantom. I thought maybe he'd say something, acknowledge me, maybe even thank me for coming. But the stage emptied. The cast disappeared. And I was left sitting there, waiting for something that never came. I finally stood, slinging my bag over my shoulder and heading for the main doors.

Then I heard it. Piano music. A slow, measured melody that carried a haunting beauty. That same eerie elegance from the night we sang in the corridors. My pulse spiked.

Was Phantom avoiding me? Hiding in some dark room, composing the next perfect aria for someone else?

Well, not this time.

I turned and followed the sound, boots clicking down the corridor, past velvet curtains and rehearsal doors until I found the room it was coming from. With my hand on the knob, I didn't hesitate.

I pushed it open, ready to confront him. But it wasn't him.

It was Nikolas.

There he sat at a glossy black piano, his back to me but still pulling me in somehow. He had an aura. His presence was strong, compelling, and impossible to ignore. I could feel his passion. He poured his soul into each note, weaving a tapestry of sound that flowed seamlessly. Each melody bleeding into the next as though they'd always belonged to him.

I paused in the doorway, mesmerized by the scene unfolding before me. I meant to leave. Meant to slip out before he noticed me. But my bag brushed against a music stand, and the sharp clang of metal shattered the air as the stand crashed to the floor with a jarring clatter.

The music halted. He turned toward me, calm and curious.

I winced, a rush of embarrassment flooding my cheeks. "Sorry," I blurted, my hands flying to my mouth. "I didn't mean to interrupt."

A small smile tugged at the corners of his lips, warm and inviting. "You're not interrupting. In fact, please come in."

I stepped into the room, quickly stooping to grab the music stand I'd knocked over. "I was just walking by," I managed, aiming for nonchalant.

He leaned back slightly, a thoughtful expression on his face. "I was wondering when we'd meet properly."

"Oh… that's right. The balcony," I said casually, like I hadn't replayed that moment in my mind countless times since.

He stood, crossed the space between us, and extended his hand. "I'm Nikolas."

Butterflies stirred within me as he approached. Up close, he was even more gorgeous than I'd expected. His eyes were intense yet impossibly warm. There was something in the way he looked at me, like he saw straight through every part of me, even the parts I usually kept hidden. I wasn't sure if that made me feel seen or exposed.

He slid his hand into mine, and for a moment, the world around us faded. We just stood there, caught in a handshake, until he gently said my name for me.

"You're Jane Norwell."

I laughed, a little embarrassed, still caught in his grip. "Sorry, yes. I'm Jane."

In a quick attempt to shift the spotlight off myself, I motioned toward the piano. "I didn't know you played."

He glanced down at the keys, a hint of nostalgia flickering in his expression. "I studied when I was younger. My mother insisted."

"Well, she was right," I said, biting back a smile, a rush of admiration threatening to spill free. "You're really good."

He motioned for me to join him on the piano bench. I hesitated, the space between us charged with a nervous energy, before finally sitting, careful not to slide too close.

"You're really good too," he said, his eyes meeting mine.

I blinked, caught off guard. "At what?"

"Good at a lot of things—dance, musical theater, teaching. You've been doing excellent work." He paused, then added, "But more than that, you make the kids believe in themselves. You make it fun. I've seen the way the kids light up around you. That's not easy to do."

My lips curved in delight, disbelief mingling with the thrill that he thought that of me. I wanted to ask when he had seen that. I hadn't noticed him at rehearsals. But part of me didn't want to ruin the moment by questioning it.

Maybe he'd been there. Maybe he just knew. Still, I couldn't help teasing.

"Should I be flattered or slightly concerned that you know all that?"

Nikolas tilted his head, playing it straight. "I see you when you're sleeping. I know when you're awake. I know when you've been bad or good..." He held the beat, then finally let a grin slip. "I'm kidding. About the sleeping part." His voice lowered, sincere now. "But I do know things. And I know you're a good person, Jane."

I swallowed. "Thank you."

I meant it and tried to say it like it was no big deal, like I wasn't suddenly blinking a little too much. But the truth clung to the edges of my thoughts.

Phantom had said I needed to push harder, that I had potential, but not quite enough. Nikolas wasn't asking me to be more. He didn't just notice me. He saw me, not as someone who needed to be fixed or shaped but as someone already doing something meaningful. Someone worth recognizing. Peter never said things like that. Not really.

Heat flooded my cheeks. "Thank you. But... musical theater doesn't exactly scream world-changing."

I wasn't trying to argue. I just wasn't used to being seen like that. Like what I did mattered.

He turned back to the keys, tapping out gentle notes. The music filled the space, steeping the room in intimacy.

"It does to me," he said. "The arts matter. That's why I host the benefit every year. It's not just about raising money—it's about honoring the work, the creativity, the effort that goes into it. I could host a charity dinner, or a sports event, but the stage is where joy comes to life. It reminds people to feel."

A glow stirred within me, recognizing the truth in his words. "I feel the same."

We sat in that moment, him improvising a beautiful tune while I watched his hands dance over the keys with fluent ease. My heart swelled with reverence, tangled with something deeper.

Then, as the final note echoed, his eyes met mine. "Come with me. I want to show you why what you do matters."

He led me away from the music rooms, and our hands brushed, his fingers grazing mine like he resisted the urge to take them. I walked just behind him, drawn forward into a quiet corridor where the lighting diffused into a twilight glow.

The walls were lined with framed photographs, showcasing past performances and handwritten scores behind glass. I followed him through the hush of it all, the sound of our footsteps swallowed by thick, royal red carpet.

At the end of the hall, we reached a heavy door set into an arched frame, its matte black surface nearly invisible in the low light.

Nikolas scanned his fingerprint, then opened the door with a light push. He stepped inside, and I followed beside him.

The room was dimly lit, the ceiling domed and dark like a planetarium. He flicked a switch, and the dome awakened, stars sparking into existence one by one until constellations stretched above us.

"This is beautiful," I breathed.

He nodded. "This is where I come for peace, to reflect, and to remember what really matters—the spirit behind everything we do." His voice carried that same warmth and certainty I was beginning to recognize as his.

He drew out a wool blanket that had been left folded by the wall.

"You just... keep a blanket in here?"

He chuckled under his breath, his gaze softening as he sat down. "It's one of my favorite places in the Palace. I come here a lot," he said, adjusting the blanket beside him. "You're welcome to join me—promise I don't bite."

That pulled a smile from me. One vampire this week had been more than enough.

I crossed the room and settled beside him, my heart racing as we sat together on the blanket, side by side beneath the planetarium sky. The ceiling glittered with soft points of light, glimmering slowly across the dome in clusters and curves. Some pulsed brighter than others, while some flickered out as quickly as they appeared.

"Are these constellations?" I asked.

Nikolas shook his head. "Not quite."

"They look like it," I murmured. "I used to love planetariums when I was a kid. I even ran the Library Science Club for a year. We'd go on field trips and try to name every star."

His mouth curved faintly. "Then you might be disappointed."

"Why?" I asked, turning to him.

He ran a hand through his hair, fingers stroking the strands back from his face, though a pale lock still fell forward, brushing his brow. I followed the motion without meaning to, my eyes tracing the shape of his lips as he spoke earnestly.

"They look like stars," he said, "but they're something else entirely. And you won't find them on any chart."

He leaned back, stretching out with one arm tucked under his head. He was completely at ease, in his element, like sharing this part of himself brought him peace. I shifted closer without meaning to. His cologne lingered between us, rich and intoxicating. His eyes met mine, and I held his gaze a second too long.

"They're emotional imprints," he said. "Grief. Joy. Wonder. Belief. Projected energy, collected from all over the world."

I looked back up, trying to make sense of the scattered patterns, but to me they were just that—patterns. Beautiful, yes, but unreadable.

"You can tell what it all means?" I asked.

He nodded.

"What does it tell you?"

"If it's safe to fly the sleigh."

I turned to the swirling lights above us. "So… what's the story behind the sleigh?" I asked. "Is there a reason you use that instead of… I don't know… a jet or a helicopter?"

Nikolas smiled, like he'd heard the question a hundred times but still liked answering it.

"There's tradition, of course, but it's more than that. Jets and helicopters need maps, long runways, and strict routes. A jet can't zigzag across rooftops or touch down on a snowy chimney without waking the whole block. The sleigh was built for this. It's faster than any aircraft and powered by something no engine could ever replicate—eight special reindeer."

"Nine," I said, grinning.

"Ah, that's right—reindeer's out of the bag. You met Garland."

"I did."

He glanced over at me. "She doesn't usually approach people. She doesn't seek the spotlight, but she's been leading the sleigh longer than any of us have been alive."

He was so comfortable and open about everything that I felt myself relax. I eased back beside him, leaning into the moment. "She really is amazing. And so is all this."

I fell silent, watching another bright cluster ripple across the dome like a breath. It was beautiful and impossibly moving. Something about this, about him, made it easy to ask the questions I'd usually hold back. I wanted to understand it all.

"So what are you looking for?" I asked. "Clear skies?"

"That's part of it," he said. "But more than anything, I'm looking for belief, kindness, and joy… even forgiveness. The atmosphere has to remain harmonious with goodness. When it does, everything aligns. And on Christmas Eve, when magic is at its peak, we have just one night to carry that spirit all around the world."

He looked at me then. "That's where you come in, Jane. That's why what you do is so important."

A quiet understanding clicked into place. I'd always known the Benefit was meant to fill hearts, lift spirits, and spread joy. In return, it not only gave to charities but also powered everything on Christmas Eve, from the sleigh to the reindeer to the deliveries.

But seeing it like this, watching how it all came together behind the scenes, was something else entirely.

We sat there, watching the stars. And I wasn't sure when it happened, but our breaths had synced, slow and steady, like a waltz to an unspoken melody.

Then a chime echoed through the starry ceiling, rippling faintly overhead. Nikolas glanced down at a small device clipped to his belt—some kind of pager, casting a soft light on his face.

"I should go," he said. "Business to attend to."

"Yeah, I should probably catch a lift before it gets too late."

He paused, looking at me. "Would you like me to send my driver or arrange a guest suite here? You'd be more than welcome."

"That's kind," I said, a little flustered. "But I've got it."

He nodded. "Well, if you ever need anything, anything at all, just ask."

He stood and offered his hand to me. My fingers slipped into his as if they were meant to fit there, and with a gentle tug, he lifted me up, stronger than I anticipated. I rose too quickly, my breath catching as I stumbled, and our bodies collided, chest to chest. His hands found my waist, firm and steady, anchoring me before the butterflies could carry me away.

The world around us faded, and for a heartbeat, we were suspended in time, neither of us daring to break the pull drawing us closer. The air crackled between us, charged with something ready to spark.

He held my gaze. "I hope to see you again soon, Jane." He gave one last lingering look before continuing. "Stay as long as you like. I trust you."

Then he turned and disappeared down one corridor, his footsteps fading into silence.

I stood there, breathless, wrapped in a dreamy haze where everything felt unreal and yet more vivid than ever.

I basked in the moment a little longer, gazing up at the shimmering lights above me. The moment was fading, but it left its imprint on me. The closeness we'd shared lingered, and something in me shifted. And deep down, I knew I'd never look at the stars the same way again.

Chapter Ten

A Candle of My Own

"**O**kay, hear me out," Celeste said, buttering a piece of toast like she was delivering a TED Talk. "You survived speed dating. You didn't combust. But now it's time—"

"To sign up for a dating app," I finished wryly.

"Yes. Just hear me out."

"I signed up last night," I said it with a small smile, careful not to sound too eager.

Celeste froze. "You what?"

I raised a hand to halt her impending excitement. "Don't start."

She grinned. "I'm not starting. I'm just pleasantly shocked. I mean, I've been trying to get you on an app for a while, and now you finally caved? And you signed up on your own? Who even are you?"

"Someone who still wants a Christmas miracle," I admitted with a shrug.

Celeste beamed. "Wow. I'm impressed."

"I have a date tonight, actually."

Celeste gawked at me like I'd just received an engagement proposal. I rolled my eyes but couldn't help smiling. "It's just one date. Don't get too excited."

"Too late!" she sang, clearly already imagining the whole wedding in her head.

I grabbed my keys and slung my coat over my arm. "Okay, I gotta get to rehearsal. Love you. Have a good day!"

In that moment, everything felt a little less stuck. My car was finally out of the shop, and I had a date tonight—another chance at love.

I didn't sign up for a dating app just because Celeste had been nudging me to, like it was the next logical step after everything. The speed dating. Dracula. Phantom. Jekyll—or Hyde, or whatever he was calling himself that night. None of it led anywhere. Not really. But I didn't sign up because I'd given up on finding love the old-fashioned way. I signed up because, for the first time in a long time, I remembered what it felt like to crave something real.

That dreamlike night under the stars with Nikolas, the tender intensity in the way he looked at me lit something I thought had gone out. I left with a warmth in my chest, feeling deeply connected in a way I hadn't felt for a long time. But still, he didn't ask. He mentioned wanting to see me again and smiled like he truly meant it, but he never actually asked. And I couldn't exactly put my heart on hold waiting for a maybe.

Christmas was practically here, with only a few days left. If I was serious about finding something real, I had to do something soon. So I downloaded the app, crafted a lighthearted profile, and matched with someone calling himself WhiteRabbit23. Tonight, I was meeting him. Just dinner. Just a first step.

He picked the restaurant, a place called *Wonder and Wine*, a cozy Wonderland-themed bistro tucked between a bookstore and a coffee shop. Nothing too theatrical, despite the name. Just mismatched chairs, twinkle lights, and tea sets repurposed as candle holders. And clocks. Clocks everywhere you looked, which felt a little ironic considering he apparently had no concept of time.

The reservation was under White R. He was supposed to arrive at 6:30 p.m. At 6:38, I checked my phone. There were no messages and no missed calls. At 6:43, I ordered a glass of Mistletoe Merlot, just to have something in front of me. At 6:50, my phone screen lit up with a new message.

White Rabbit: "Terribly sorry! Running just a bit behind! Five minutes, I promise!"

I stared at the screen, letting the words sink in. After a moment, I replied with a simple, "No worries."

I wasn't angry. Not quite. I was just tired. Tired of pouring hope into empty promises. Tired of squeezing myself into a dress and pretending that this time might end differently.

By the thirty-minute mark, I was halfway through drafting a sarcastic text to White Rabbit when a new message flashed across my screen.

Dracula: "Thinking about you. Want some company?"

I stared at the message, a mixture of emotions swirling within me. For a fleeting second, the idea of being wanted felt nice, and I even considered taking him up on his invitation. But Dracula wasn't the one for me—I knew that. And I'd rather be alone than be with someone, anyone, who wasn't right for me. A quiet realization stirred in me. For once, I felt okay being alone—not because I was giving up on love, but because I might finally be okay with my own company.

The waiter stopped by my table. "Still expecting someone?"

I exhaled, keeping my tone light. "I think he's chasing a clock somewhere."

The waiter nodded like he'd heard it all before. "Would you like to order anyway?"

I did. And when the food came, I ate slowly and alone. I'd seen people like this before, sitting solo at candlelit tables, nursing a drink or picking at their dinner with quiet focus. I used to wonder about their stories. Were they waiting for someone? Had they been stood up? Were they simply… lonely?

Maybe some of them had been. Maybe some of them were exactly where I was now. But the thing I never realized until this moment was that they weren't broken. They weren't tragic. They were resilient. It took strength to stay seated. To be present. To breathe through disappointment and still savor the wine.

And now that I was here, I didn't feel foolish or embarrassed. I felt like maybe I was stronger than I'd given myself credit for. I stayed present in the moment, enjoying the mellow hum of music, the gentle clinking of silverware, and the warm firelight of a candle that belonged entirely to me.

I watched the people outside the window, took slow sips, and let my mind wander. For once, it didn't spiral. It settled. And in that calm came a simple truth: I was just me. Not magical or remarkable in any obvious way, and certainly not the most dazzling person in the room. I was just human—complicated, kind, inconsistent. I might not be extraordinary in the way this world seemed to reward, but I was real. I was me. And that was okay.

By the time I paid the bill, the night had come to a bittersweet close. I was just about to slip out when a woman's voice called across the room.

"Miss Norwell?"

The voice was surprised. I looked up to find a couple beside my table, the woman's kind eyes bright with recognition. Her husband hovered behind her, offering a courteous nod of greeting.

"I'm sorry," I said, trying to place them.

"You probably don't remember us," the woman said quickly. "We're the Dawsons. Our daughter, Sophie, had you some years ago in sixth grade musical theater."

Sophie. It took a second, but then it clicked. The shy girl with the surprisingly big voice. I remembered her.

"Oh, yes! Wow, that feels like a lifetime ago," I said, rising from my seat.

"We just saw you from across the room and had to say something. Sophie just got accepted into Juilliard."

A swell of joy rose through me. "Wow. Juilliard. That's amazing. I'm so happy for her."

Pride gleamed in her eyes. "She's still in shock. But she never would've had the confidence to apply if it weren't for you. You always believed in her. You pushed her just enough without scaring her off. She still talks about you."

"She says she sings because of you," the man added. "We just wanted to say thank you."

I felt a lump form in my throat, blinking back unexpected tears. "Thank you," I managed. "That really means a lot."

They looked at me with genuine kindness before drifting back into the crowd.

As I stepped out of the restaurant, snowflakes drifted down around me, settling over me like the Dawsons' words. They echoed in my mind, uplifting and steady, like a presence I could lean on. I had spent so long focusing on my own romantic misfires that I'd forgotten the power of the little things—the ways we touch

93

people's lives, even if just in small measures. Being remembered reminded me of that. Not because I needed it to feel seen, but because it showed I already had been. In a world that often felt so big and daunting, I realized I had a place in it—one that was mine alone.

I walked slowly, aware of how different I felt from when the night began. This wasn't the evening I had imagined when I signed up for the dating app, but somehow, it felt right. As I reached my car, I pulled out my phone, half-expecting to see another message from White Rabbit.

But there was nothing. And that was okay.

The car ride home felt different. Instead of the familiar hum of uncertainty and self-doubt, I felt lighter, buoyed by the unexpected encounter. I turned up the music, letting the notes fill the space around me, and I sang along—not caring if I hit every note perfectly, not trying to come out of my shell or "stop hiding." I was just being me. And it was liberating.

When I got home, I kicked off my shoes and sank into bed, the smooth fabric cradling me as I pulled a blanket over myself. My thoughts drifted to my students, to my passions, to everything that made me feel alive. I thought of Sophie and the gift of encouragement I had unknowingly given her.

That's when I realized the miracle I'd been searching for wasn't in a romantic partner or a whirlwind of passion. It was in connections to others, to myself, and to the moments that made life extraordinary, even in their simplicity.

As I settled into the quiet of Celeste's guest room, my gaze landed on the framed photos lining the dresser: Celeste and Henry at their wedding, Penny grinning in a Halloween costume, Mom and Dad from a Christmas long ago. In the center was a photo from last year's tree lighting, all of us bundled in scarves, arms linked and cheeks rosy from the cold, caught mid-laugh in the twinkle of holiday lights.

A sense of hope bloomed within me, steady and true. Love came in many forms. It was okay to want romance, but it was also okay to embrace the love that already surrounded me. I was not alone. I was part of a tapestry of lives that intertwined, each thread vibrant and valuable.

I rolled over to shut off the lamp, and a moment later, I felt the bed shift. Princess Butterscotch nudged her way into a nook beside me. Comfort eased through me as I petted her, and she snuggled closer like she understood.

"Goodnight," I whispered softly.

Whatever the coming days held, I was ready. I was centered. And that was enough.

Chapter Eleven
Comfort and Joy

Monday's dress rehearsal came and went too quickly. Now it was Christmas Eve—the day of the benefit. The halls had been buzzing since morning, filled with laughter and the kind of joy that felt like it could float. The performance was everything we'd worked for. The kids nailed it. The crowd cheered. And for the first time in a long time, it felt like Christmas.

I thought I knew what to expect after this weekend's run-through and yesterday's dress rehearsal. But nothing compared to tonight. It's funny how that happens. You think you've seen it all, and then the day arrives. The lights come on, the music starts, and suddenly it's real. Everything feels bigger. More marvelous than I could've imagined.

I had watched the broadcast in years past, curled up on my couch, wishing I was there. And tonight, I was backstage. I was part of it. Watching my students light up under those stage lights and seeing their nerves melt into joy felt like a special kind of happiness. And hearing the applause swell after their final pose? I'll never forget it, and I don't think they will either.

Backstage was chaos in the best way, with glitter on the floor, kids humming with excitement, and people hugging like it was the last day of school.

Celeste found me first, with Penny right beside her, bright-eyed and beaming.

"You did such a great job," Celeste said, pulling me into a hug. "Seriously. That whole show, your group, everything was incredible."

Penny threw her arms around us, squeezing in tight. "Your kids were the best ones, Aunt Jane. You made the show."

My chest tightened as I held them both close. "Thank you. Love you both."

"Love you too," Celeste said, brushing her hand gently along my back. "Henry's pulling the car around. We'll head out. We still have lots of cookies to bake before dinner. See you at home soon."

"I'll be home in time to finish the mashed potatoes," I promised.

I watched them go, warmth blooming in my chest as they slipped back into the crowd. I stood there for a moment, not quite ready for the night to end. The crowd moved around me, but for a second, everything felt still—and there he was. Nikolas, standing just offstage, speaking with a small group of donors. He looked sharp, captivating in a way that made it hard to look away. Across the bustle, his eyes found mine—steady, like I was the only one in the room. Even in a crowd, even when I felt invisible to everyone else, somehow he always looked right at me. Just like that day on the balcony.

My heart fluttered. I didn't want it to, but it did. I'd just come to terms with being alone—that I didn't need a relationship to feel whole, that I was enough. And I'd meant it. I really had. So why was I suddenly struggling to breathe? Why did it feel like something had cracked open in me, just from the way he looked at me? Was I imagining that connection? Was I reading too much into the way it felt that night under the stars, the way he opened up, like he trusted me with something fragile. He brought me into his world. He told me what he saw in me, even the parts I wasn't sure I believed myself. But most of all, there was the way he looked at me. The way our breaths fell into the same rhythm. It felt magnetic. Real. It still did.

I blinked back into the moment. Across the room, he was still watching me. He smiled, soft, deliberate, and a little knowing. And for a moment, it felt like he answered the question I'd just asked myself.

I smiled back, a little breathless. Then someone touched his arm, and his focus returned to the conversation. And just like that, he was gone again.

I stayed a few minutes longer—hugged a few parents and thanked the crew. I paused, taking one last look back at the Palace before heading out.

The sun had just set, casting a dusky hue over the rooftops as I stepped outside and boarded the staff shuttle.

A few minutes later, the shuttle eased into the staff lot and the doors whooshed open. People trickled off, heading toward their cars under the cast of the garage lights. I slid into the driver's seat and exhaled. It was over. The show, the night, the whirlwind of it all. But more than anything, there was Nikolas. And I couldn't ignore the ache I felt, knowing I didn't get to say goodbye.

I stared through the windshield for a moment, hoping for something. I didn't even know what. I sighed and turned the key. Nothing. I tried again, but all I got was a dull click and a weak blink from the dash.

"You've got to be kidding me." I slumped forward, resting my forehead against the steering wheel. "Not tonight…"

I stayed like that for a moment, breathing in the silence, trying to hold back the frustration. With a quiet sigh, I opened the door and stepped out, glancing around the lot. The place was nearly empty now, and the stillness carried a weight of its own.

That's when I heard the low hum of an engine. A glossy black Porsche swept through the garage. It pulled up beside my car and rolled to a smooth stop. The window lowered.

Nikolas.

"Everything alright?" he asked.

I straightened, brushing hair from my face. "Car trouble. Again."

He watched me for a beat, concern flickering in his expression. "That's frustrating. Want me to work a little magic?"

Something about the way he said it felt so sincere and careful, as though he didn't want to overstep. Like he genuinely wanted to help. Like he'd fix the whole night, but only if I let him.

But Celeste had already tried earlier this week—twice. Whatever was wrong with it wasn't budging. Still, a tiny part of me wondered if Nikolas actually could fix it with a touch. I just didn't want him to remember me like this—standing beside a dying car in the middle of an empty garage, looking like a walking problem.

"No, it's okay," I said, lifting my chin a little. "I think it's just… done."

He didn't push. There was understanding in his eyes, as if he knew exactly why I'd said no.

"I was hoping I'd catch you," he said, stepping out of the Porsche, composed and collected. Time seemed to slow as he rounded the front of the car and closed the space between us. "I didn't get to tell you how amazing you were tonight."

I was momentarily speechless before I could answer. "...
Thank you."

His eyes lingered on mine. "If you need a ride, I'd be happy
to take you myself."

I hesitated, not because I didn't want to go, but because
spending more time with him meant the goodbye waiting at the
end would be even harder. Still, I couldn't bring myself to walk
away, not when every part of me wanted just a little more time.

"I'd like that," I said, heart thudding as I moved to join him.

He looked pleased as he opened the passenger door for me,
thoughtful and intentional, like it meant something. And it did.

As I slid into the seat, he gave me a once-over, his lips curving
slightly. "You look nice tonight. Is that a dress or pants?"

The fabric flowed like a gown, and I couldn't blame him for
asking.

"Pants," I said, smoothing the wide-leg hem as I settled in.

"Good," he said, his eyes holding a playful intensity, like he
knew something I didn't.

My head turned. "Why?"

But he just smiled, closed the door, and made his way back
around to the driver's side. I let it go. For now.

The Porsche purred to life, impossibly smooth and luxurious.
He drove us smoothly through the lower level of the garage,
winding past rows of gleaming high-end vehicles until we reached
a far corner I hadn't even realized existed.

Nikolas tapped something on the center console. A set of
heavy double doors ahead of us hissed open slowly. Behind them
was... an elevator. A vehicle-sized lift bathed in a soft amber light.

"You have a private car elevator?" I asked, eyebrows raised.

Nikolas just gave me a look as if that was the least impressive
thing he had up his sleeve. The Porsche eased inside. The doors

sealed shut behind us, and a moment later, I felt the subtle shift as we began to rise.

His hand rested easily on the gear shift as he turned to me, then asked, "Do you trust me?"

"Yes," I breathed.

He looked pleased by my answer as the car ascended.

"The benefit was a success. One of the best we've had," he said. "I think you had a lot to do with that."

Heat rose to my cheeks. "I had a good group. They know how to light up a room. It was all them."

He held my gaze. "Some people light up a room," he said. "You steady it."

He paused as if the rest didn't need saying, but said it anyway. "There's something real in that."

For a second, I couldn't speak. His words settled deep—unexpected and achingly moving. I didn't reply, but I didn't need to. The silence between us held tender and light, a perfect blend of comfort and joy.

The elevator climbed higher. I watched the numbers tick upward, past the main lobby, past the Opera House, the staff quarters, and everything I'd walked through and memorized. I couldn't see any of it now, but I felt it—each level lifting us higher, rising further into something unknown.

Then the doors slid open ahead of us, and the sky was right there—endless and ink-black. A rooftop, vast and flat, veiled in an ethereal haze.

Nikolas shifted into drive and eased us forward, out of the elevator and onto the open roof. Wind swept across the rooftop, carrying flecks of snow with it. And waiting at the center was a sleigh. Not just any sleigh. His sleigh.

The reindeer stood at attention, their breath curling in small clouds, harnesses catching the light. Garland's antlers glowed with a luminous brilliance, casting a gentle glimmer across the night sky. The sleigh sat under the golden glow, regal and dreamy.

Nikolas turned to me and asked, "Are you ready?"

My heart leapt into my throat as we stepped out of the car. The city glittered below us, thousands of lights shimmering. The rooftop stretched out before us. No walls, no rails. Just wind, snow, and the impossible reality of what we were about to do.

I followed him toward the sleigh, boots crunching lightly on the soft snow. It felt like another world—unlike anything I'd ever known. As we approached, Garland looked toward me, her eyes meeting mine.

"It's lovely weather for a sleigh ride," she said.

A quiet amazement swept through me as I took it all in. The sleigh was beautiful, classic in silhouette, with elegant wooden runners and a deep red body, the kind you'd see on the front of a Christmas card.

But as we got closer, the details shifted. The seat wasn't a bench or split into sections. It was a single seat, narrow and intimate, just long enough for one to sit in front and another to settle in closely behind. It had the sumptuous upholstery of a luxury car's interior and was shaped to cradle its riders in close comfort beneath the stars.

I tilted my head. "There's no second seat?"

I glanced toward the back, where a low, open compartment curved like a bench.

Nikolas caught my glance, a smile forming on his lips. "The back's not built for sitting. It's for toys."

I peered in again. "Doesn't look like a billion toys could fit back there."

A glint of amusement touched his eyes. "It does when I'm driving," he said, climbing in first, settling into the seat like he was born for it.

His gaze lingered on me, intent and inviting. "Climb in."

A shiver of anticipation ran through me. I'd never ridden in a sleigh before, not like this. But I moved without thinking, drawn in by the warmth in his voice and the shimmer of the sleigh. I slipped in behind him, legs straddling his. And all at once, I understood the pants comment.

The seat was snug. Warmer than I expected. Or maybe it was just the heat of the moment. I was wrapped around him, held close by the fit of the seat and the nearness of his body. He reached behind and took my hands, guiding them around his waist.

"Hold on tight," he said.

For a second, everything was still. Just the two of us, nestled in the sleigh, close and cozy, my arms wrapped around him, the world holding its breath. Then the sleigh bolted forward in a burst of speed so sudden that I yelped, giggling as cold air rushed past my face, my hair whipping wildly behind me. I clung to him, my arms tightening instinctively around his waist, my cheek snug against his shoulder.

The reindeer soared. The runners scraped the floor once, then caught the wind, and suddenly, we lifted. Up. Higher. The ground dropped away in one graceful swoop, and suddenly, we were flying, soaring through the open sky.

I squeezed my eyes shut, overwhelmed by the rush, but opened them a second later, not wanting to let a single moment slip away. It was breathtakingly fast, but exhilarating.

The sleigh leveled as we climbed higher, gliding smoothly above the rooftops. The wind softened. The motion steadied. I let out a breath I hadn't realized I'd been holding. Everything slowed—we were floating, gliding over the city, snow around us like glitter suspended in time.

Nikolas glanced back over his shoulder. "You okay?"

"Yes," I murmured against his shoulder, holding him tighter.

I was more than okay. I was floating—in more ways than one. The sky wrapped around us like velvet. The world below faded into golden specks. And all I could feel was his warmth, his presence strong and steady in front of me as our breaths threaded into the same rhythm again.

For a moment, I let myself believe it could stay this way forever. But as we glided lower, the clouds gave way to moonlit rooftops. The familiar grid of Snow Bridge began to take shape beneath us, brownstones and houses lined in neat rows, their streets illuminated by the orange light of old streetlamps.

Then I saw it. Our street. Our house. The one with the string of candy cane lights and Penny's snowman still standing proudly on the lawn, his red hat slightly crooked. We were almost home. My heart ached. I didn't want this to end. I didn't want him to go. Not yet.

The sleigh glided to a gentle stop, the runners brushing softly against the snow as the reindeer's hooves settled against the pavement, light as snowfall. The night was hushed, the kind of silent night that only Christmas Eve could bring. Beyond the quiet streets, soft light spilled from the windows of nearby homes, shadows shifting where families gathered together in the glow of tables and hearths.

We landed right in front of the house. Nikolas stepped down from the sleigh, then turned and reached for me. He took my hand, guiding me down from the sleigh. My heart raced as the space between us vanished. He drew me close, his hand still in mine. Our faces… inches apart. I could feel his breath on my lips, achingly close.

I didn't move. Neither did he. We just stood there, the air between us thinning with every breath. My heart was thudding so hard, I was sure he could hear it. His eyes dropped to my lips, and mine did the same. Our mouths were so close I could almost taste the moment. And then—

"Santa? Reindeer? Aunt Jane?"

We both turned. There she was, Penny, still in her dress from the benefit, standing on the porch in her house shoes. The moment between me and Nikolas slipped away, melting between us like snow. I blinked. "Penny, what are you doing out here? Where are your boots? Your coat?"

Penny didn't answer. In seconds, she was at the curb, taking it all in—Garland, the antlers, the shimmer of bells. Her eyes sparkled as she turned to Nikolas. "Do you have something for me?" she asked, her voiced hushed with wonder.

I lifted her into my arms before her toes could freeze. "It's not time yet," I said softly.

Nikolas smiled. "Of course I have something special for you. But I need to be across the ocean in... twenty-seven minutes. I'll return later, when the chimney's cool and not a creature is stirring, not even Princess Butterscotch."

Penny's eyes lit up. "You know Princess Butterscotch?"

He nodded. "And I just might have something special for her too."

Then he looked at me, full of things he didn't say, and climbed into the sleigh.

A swirl of velvet. The jingle of bells. Then they were gone, rising into the sky until even Garland's glowing antlers vanished into the stars.

Penny looked to the sky, to the place where the sleigh had disappeared. "Do you think he'll really come back?" she asked, her voice full of hope.

I looked up too, still holding onto the feeling. "I think anything's possible tonight," I said. And with Penny in my arms, we stepped inside.

The house wasn't full of family—just me, Celeste, Penny, Henry, and Princess Butterscotch, but it was full of love. Full of chaos in the best way—the real, messy, human kind of Christmas Eve. Crumpled wrapping paper, carols playing on a loop, too much sugar, spilled hot chocolate, and a little glitter stuck to everything.

We ate too much. We laughed even more. Penny tore through her early gifts like a tornado in tinsel. Someone started a dance-off in the living room, and Christmas karaoke followed. I was in the middle of it all, smiling on the outside. Inside, though, there was this gentle ache. Not sadness, not really. Just that feeling when you're surrounded by love but still aware of the space beside you that isn't filled.

I didn't say much about the Palace, or the sleigh, or the moment in the front yard. It all felt too fragile to put into words, like saying it aloud might make it disappear.

Later, after the chaos settled into yawns and bedtime stories, after the dishwasher hummed and Henry put out the fire in the fireplace, I stayed downstairs, curled up in the living room—the one with the chimney and the biggest window. Celeste found me still sitting there.

"You heading to bed?" she asked, already in slippers, her hair pulled back.

I shook my head. "Not tired."

She didn't press. She just gave me a look of quiet understanding, the kind you give someone when you know exactly what they're waiting for, and you love them enough not to say it out loud.

I pulled a blanket over my lap and cradled a steaming mug of cocoa, my eyes drifting between the fireplace and the sky beyond the window. I tried to stay awake. I blinked hard. I took slow sips of cocoa. I even hummed my favorite carols. But the Sandman must've sprinkled something extra in the air tonight. Sleep was winning. I could feel it tugging at me harder than I wanted to admit. I wasn't built like him. Nikolas. He didn't stop. Not in December. He worked through the night, carrying the weight of joy and wonder like the whole season depended on it—because it did. He was built for this. For giving everything he had, even when no one was there to see it.

I watched the stars for as long as I could, just in case. But eventually, I drifted off.

Chapter Twelve
Christmas Day

Morning came quietly. No sleigh bells. No chimney thuds. Just early sunlight filtering through the curtains and the faint hum of life returning to normal.

I sat up slowly, eyes drifting toward the fireplace. The stockings were full. The plate of cookies was empty. Beneath the tree, a sea of carefully wrapped gifts glittered in the gentle morning light—more than any of us had left there the night before.

He'd come. And I'd missed him.

I let out a long, deep breath. I wasn't even sure what I'd expected. To wake up and find him sitting beside me? A whispered promise to stay? Something, anything, to say he hadn't wanted to leave.

My eyes moved to the tree, tall and lush, branches heavy with glass ornaments and silver ribbon, shimmering softly from the string lights woven through. It looked like something out of a fairytale.

Beneath it all, one box caught my eye. Wrapped in gold paper and tied with red thread, it was set just slightly forward from the others—deliberate and certain, as if it had been placed for this very moment. My name was written across the top, waiting patiently for me to wake up and find it. I reached for it, a flutter rising in my chest as I held it, taking the moment in before opening it.

Inside lay a vintage musical jewelry box. Pale pink lacquer shimmered with a satin finish, and its gold hinges caught the light. This was no ordinary jewelry box. It was a treasure from the past that stirred something deep within me. Hand-painted scenes from the Nutcracker danced along the sides, each brushstroke pulling me back to a beautiful memory of childhood.

I lifted the lid, and the soft, aching notes of the "Pas de Deux" filled the air—rich, romantic, and full of longing. The music wrapped around me like a familiar embrace. A delicate ballerina twirled gracefully in place, lost in her own enchanted world.

A gentle warmth filled my heart. For a moment, I was transported back to a time when anything felt possible, promises felt like forever, and I believed that nothing precious ever truly disappeared.

I'd had one just like it when I was little. It broke during a move, cracked down the middle as if it couldn't survive the transition. I cried harder over that silly jewelry box than I did over my first breakup. It wasn't expensive, but it had meant something. It had meant everything.

I never told Nikolas that. But somehow… he knew.

I traced the edge with trembling fingers, then noticed a small card tucked beneath the velvet lining.

For the girl who moves through life like a quiet waltz—steady, graceful, unforgettable.

My eyes welled, the words hitting deeper than I expected. I stood in front of the tree, the jewelry box held close to my chest, its song still playing in the quiet. I smiled, but my heart sank, just a little. Maybe that was all it was ever meant to be, a perfect night, a once-in-a-lifetime kind of magic.

The melody floated into the stillness, fading like a breath. Then came the sound of familiar footsteps. Penny rushed past in her elf pajamas, squealing as she dove toward her presents. Wrapping paper flew in every direction as she tore through them with glee.

Henry followed with a cheerful "Ho ho ho!" and a Santa hat that looked like it was trying to escape from his head. Celeste beamed, her eyes filled with delight at the chaos. I smiled too, wished them a "Merry Christmas," and offered to take Princess Butterscotch out for a walk.

I just needed a minute to breathe, to think, to feel everything and let it settle. So I bundled up, clipped on Princess Butterscotch's leash, and stepped outside.

The neighborhood was serene in the early light of Christmas morning. Snow blanketed the rooftops and hedges, sparkling like diamonds in the morning sun. A few red birds flitted from branch to branch, their calls threading through the silence. I walked slowly, trying not to think about anything in particular.

We turned the corner, and Princess Butterscotch trotted ahead like she'd never seen snow before—pawing at a lumpy snowbank, sniffing at tiny snowflakes, and investigating every mailbox, fencepost, and bootprint along the way.

As we neared our house again, something shifted in the air. Her ears perked. Then she let out a sudden bark and tugged hard, her leash snapping taut as she pulled me forward.

"Okay, okay," I laughed, jogging to keep up. "You're not even that athletic—what's gotten into you?"

She bolted toward the front yard, her tail wagging with un-containable excitement. Nikolas was standing at the edge of the front yard, framed by snow-covered hedges and morning light.

He wore a deep, wintry red coat, expertly tailored and buttoned to the top. His hands were tucked patiently in his pockets, his eyes steady on me. A flood of emotion rushed through me as I realized he'd come back.

Princess Butterscotch bounded right up to him, tail wagging as she gave a few enthusiastic sniffs before trotting back to my side, satisfied as if she'd just given her approval.

Nikolas gave me a tender look, warming me from the cold like a flickering fire. "Sorry I missed you," he said. "Had a few billion stops to make."

I stepped closer, heart thudding against my ribs, each beat echoing the unspoken longing between us. "I was hoping you'd come back."

His gaze held a contentment, as though being here was enough. "You didn't think I'd let Christmas go by without seeing you, did you?"

Joy swelled inside me, quiet but fierce. "No," I murmured. "Not really."

He stepped closer, closing the distance, his gaze unwavering. "Good," he said. "Because I couldn't stay away from you."

Sparks ignited in my chest. We held each other's eyes, the world fading around us.

"I don't know what happens next," he said. "But I'd really like to find out with you."

My breath caught, my lips parting in a soft bloom of agreement. "I'd like that too."

His expression deepened, and something undeniable surged between us. He moved even closer, and everything else fell away. As he leaned in, I knew this was it. The moment I had been longing for since the first time I laid eyes on him. The almost that had lived in every look and every pause. The kiss we hadn't finished, the one that had hovered between us all night. Now it was here—finally, fully here. His hand found my cheek, fingers trailing gently along my jaw before caressing the curve of my lips. Then he kissed me, slow and certain, as if he had been holding back forever.

His lips were warm, tasting faintly of winter bliss and something deliciously his own. My hands curled into the fabric of his coat, anchoring me in that intoxicating moment. His hand slipped to the small of my back, pulling me in until there was no space left between us. We lingered in that closeness, my heart overflowing, as we savored the intimacy of the moment. We finally pulled back—not far, just enough to catch our breath, our foreheads resting together.

"Merry Christmas," he whispered.

"Merry Christmas," I whispered back. And this time, it felt like mine.

"Come on," he said. "There's one more thing."

I followed him, still a little dizzy from the kiss. Princess Butterscotch trotted along beside us. When we rounded the side of the house, a sleek black car waited in the driveway, shiny and spotless with a giant red bow on top.

I blinked. "Wait… what's that?"

Nikolas smiled. "Just something a little more reliable."

He reached into his coat and handed me a key fob. I stared down at it, then back at the car. It was beautiful and timeless, far nicer than anything I would've ever let myself have. But it felt perfect. I swallowed hard, a wave of disbelief washing over me. "This is too much."

"It's just enough," he said.

Nikolas walked ahead and opened the driver's side door for me, a spark of delight in his eyes. "Shall we?"

"Yes," I breathed as I slid into the seat. My hands wrapped around the wheel—smooth, solid, and mine.

Princess Butterscotch hopped into the back like she already knew where we were headed. Nikolas closed the door, then circled around and climbed into the passenger seat.

"Thank you," I said, excitement and gratitude tangling together.

He looked at me, certainty in his gaze. "Anything for you."

He watched me, as if my joy was the highlight of his day.

I pressed the start button. The engine hummed to life beneath my hands, and something in me did too.

We cruised through the quiet streets, everything hushed yet still humming with that holiday spirit. We stopped for coffee at the only café open on Christmas Day, just the two of us in our own little pocket of joy, before heading back to Celeste's, ready to share that joy with everyone waiting inside.

We hadn't called it a date. There was no label, no plan, no rules. But Nikolas stayed with me the whole day. He carried the weight of the season on his shoulders while still making room for me. And in that space, something real was growing.

And somewhere between the second helping of my mashed potatoes and watching him laugh across the table with Celeste and Henry, Penny giggling between them, it hit me. This was a date. The twelfth one, actually.

I had been on twelve dates in twelve days. And somehow, the one that wasn't planned felt like the only one that ever truly mattered. I ended up finding someone special for Christmas after all. Or more like… someone special found me.

And from that moment on, I knew I'd never go through another Christmas feeling like something was missing.

The End

Mia Reign Miller
Author of The 12th Date

Mia Reign Miller is a writer and former stage performer whose love of dance, theatre, and timeless romance inspires her storytelling. She writes uplifting tales with warmth, wonder, and a touch of magic. *The 12th Date* is her debut publication, with more heartfelt stories on the way.

Thank you for spending part of your holiday season with Jane and Nikolas.

If this story brought you warmth, wonder, or even a bit of magic, I'd be deeply grateful if you shared a review.

Every kind word helps this story find its way to another heart.

More tales are on the horizon — new worlds, new voices, and journeys I can't wait to share.

Stay connected or hear about the next release:
Evergrove Media

- Email: contact@evergrovemedia.com
- TikTok: @evergrove.media
- Instagram: @evergrove.media
- linktr.ee/evergrove.media

With gratitude,
Mia Reign Miller

www.ingramcontent.com/pod-product-compliance
Lightning Source LLC
Chambersburg PA
CBHW021926170626
46807CB00007B/3006